MW01135542

The Wind is my Messenger

Jack E. Tetirick

Writers Club Press

San Jose New York Lincoln Shanghai

The Wind is My Messenger

Published by Writers Club Press
an imprint of iUniverse.com, Inc.

This is a work of pure fiction. Any resemblance to any person
living or deadis accidental, coincidental, and unintentional. The science
is also fiction,but hopefully, not for very long.

For information address:
iUniverse.com, Inc.
620 North 48th Street
Suite 201
Lincoln, NE 68504-3467
www.iuniverse.com

ISBN: 0-595-00168-8

Printed in the United States of America

For Kelly

CONTENTS

I wish to acknowledge the support
and patience of my wife.

*S*cience is a dream made real.
Faith is trust made manifest.

AN OLYMPIC PRODIGY

I love my morning shower. Especially after Pearce, a coach…a sadist is more like it around women athletes…has spent all afternoon running me up and down the steps at Memorial Stadium until my legs wobble like wet noodles. Pushed me back against the brick wall for his stretch-split special until my you-know-what is two inches from the blacktop. Next, a waist-bend forcing my head between my knees for a view of my butt and the bright blue sky beyond. That is until his simple upside-down face appears, blond wispy hair blowing, translucent ears glowing and that stupid permanent smile. "Way to go Toni! One more time up the steps, *Okay?*"

Can you believe it? The Boston Globe gave *him* the credit for my downhill Bronze three years ago. That's right. Sheely, in his big-deal "Sports Today" column claimed a genius Harvard track coach made a downhill ski champion out of a seventeen-year-old. Never mind I had won every downhill in New England before I even met Pearce. But according to Sheely, I was so much putty until *The Coach* taught me wind sprints. What bullshit. A *track* coach. Pearce couldn't stand up on a bunny slope. But that's what sportswriters are paid to do, isn't it?

1

I turned the water scalding hot and did deep knee bends facing into the torrent. The muscles were rivers of fire, front and back, but the stiffness had faded, all but the left hamstring, still touchy from yanking my leg when I missed a gate at Park City. I slid my fingertips down gingerly from the crease of my butt to the back of my knee. It felt like I was slicing my leg open with a knife, but the tortured muscle as hard as a rock…my Welsh ancestor's leg muscles. Those legs have won me a lot of downhills. And they're not that bad to look at either. I'm no thunder-thighs like Heidi Fleisch, more like a race horse. Which is what Pearce thinks I am. He thinks he owns a race horse. I bent over, letting the water burn a hot river down my back and run off of my hair hanging over the drain. I snapped off the water, stepped out onto the thick cotton pile and yanked a large white fluffy towel from the rack.

I dried quickly and walked out into the long hallway that fronts the length of the house on the top floor. Naked as the day I was born, I flipped the huge towel to cover here and there.

My father entered the hallway from his bedroom at the far end of the hall. He wore razor-creased striped morning trousers, a dark coat over a snowy white shirt, and a dark wine-colored silk tie. I will say this, Bernard Putnam III is every inch an aristocrat, tall and craggy with unruly black hair, a pale narrow face with deep-set blue eyes and a very heavy beard. He shaves twice on any day when he is to be out in the evening. He glanced nervously out of the windows fronting the hallway as he walked toward me.

"Toni," he said, after a close inspection, "when are we going to get you to stop running around half-naked?" His voice was more teasing than serious.

I twined my arms up around his neck, hugging him and kissing a cheek scraped raw. His clothes always seemed rough and warm.

"You love it, Barney, you love it," I said. I pushed back, brushed away some drops of water from a spotless lapel and patted the cheek where I had just kissed him. "You look like the owner of a funeral parlor."

"And you, Toni, are quite simply the most beautiful woman I've ever seen." He paused. He hates to show emotion. "It is, of course, all due to your lovely mother, certainly not the Putnams, who were, and are, decidedly ugly."

"Well, Barney, I have your height, see? My nose is right under your big chin. And I have your beard!" I held up my arm, displaying the thick black tuft of hair. Barney stared at it. It made me think he was waiting for the hair in my armpit to suddenly split apart and the Devil to peer out. The church clothes added to the impression.

He shook his head and made a face. "Do you have *any* idea how much that bothers your mother, Toni? She would prefer having a serial killer in the family. She's never mentioned your refusal to shave…there, since that terrible argument. I swear she never has. But you and I both know the greatest kindness you could ever have for her would be to shave that stuff off."

There would be no shaving or anything else. I turned away into my bedroom. "See you below, Papa. I'm hungry enough to eat a boiled owl. Tell Lucille I want three poached eggs on toast, four slices of that good Danish ham, and a carload of coffee."

The eggs were waiting, just arrived, as I slid into my seat. At the head of the table Jeanette was also dressed for church, but she had slipped a pale natural cashmere sweater over her dark amber dress. The second floor dining room ceiling was fourteen feet high to accommodate a crystal chandelier, and was always chilly on early spring mornings. My mother never complained about it. She loved her three story Louisburg Square apartment, its worm-eaten woodwork, drafty bedrooms, and ancient dumbwaiter creaking up from the first floor kitchen. She was right. It was a lovely antique, fronted by a cobblestone walkway where discrete neighbors always reliably scooped up after their pets.

Barney was reading the Sunday edition of the New York Times, delivered faithfully by the night watchman from the bank.

"I take it you're not going with us?" Jeanette asked, eyeing my jeans and blue-striped sailor's knit. She looked regal as well as lovely. She always seemed about to smile, but she rarely did.

"Who's preaching, Cotton Mather?"

"Waldo Emerson," said Barney. "Harvard seniors are noted for their snottiness," he said to Jeanette.

"Mother, I'm going up to the gym to work out. Then I have to check all of my stuff so Pearce can get it out to Logan. Then pack. The plane goes out tomorrow at noon." I sliced up my eggs and attacked them hungrily. "I'm worried about my left hamstring. I hit a flag out at Park City and when I yanked my ski back, it hurt like hell, and still does."

"Toni, don't swear!" Jeanette said. She was edgy. She detests flying, especially over water, rarely returning to France to see her family despite Barney's frequent business trips to the Union Bank of Switzerland. "You travel too much." I'd heard this lecture many times. "I really don't care for all of this skiing, anyway," she fretted. "It's dangerous, and some of the people are tramps."

"Take it easy, Jeannie," argued Barney quietly. "It's spring break. She's earned it. Her grades show it. There'll be a whole plane-load of kids, both the participants as well as the spectators. The festival at Davos is a lot of fun and not too serious. Don't spoil it...I"

"Toni," my mother interrupted, "Huff is going with you? I'm right about that, am I not?"

"Try and leave him behind," I replied sarcastically as I stuffed my mouth with ham.

Jeanette Putnam stabbed at a slice of grapefruit with a tiny silver spoon. "That's exactly what I mean about bad manners, Toni! Huff Lawrence puts you up on a pedestal, and you lash at him with remarks like that. Insufferable manners. You know it!"

"He loves it."

"No one likes being treated like an idiot, Toni. You're going to lose him one of these days."

"I can only hope."

"What in the world is wrong with Huff, Toni, he is good looking…"

"And very rich,"

"He treats you like a princess, always has since you were children. And wasn't he some sort of corner back, or whatever you call it at Harvard, before he went off to law school? Isn't all that sweat and struggle what stirs you up so much?"

"He was a quarterback, not a corner back."

"Oh well, what's the difference…what I…"

"A quarterback gets to put his hands under the center's butt, mother, before he gets the ball. If a corner back touches anybody's butt, he gets a penalty…a yellow flag."

Jeanette looked over at her husband, who was deep into the newspaper.

"I don't appreciate vulgarity either," she replied.

"He was a lousy quarterback. Plenty of talent, no fire. Couldn't care less…Mother, Hughes bought first class tickets for us on Swissair. I made him change them to tourist. He has trouble understanding."

"Well, so do I. I thought you wanted to be rested when you arrive. I'm sure that's what he had in mind."

"Mother, I have *friends* on that airplane. People from all over the country in all kinds of winter sports. Some of them can't even buy their equipment! And you and Hughes Lawrence want me sitting up in first class where my friends can't even use the toilet?"

My father closed his newspaper. "Has anyone checked that muscle, Toni?" he asked.

"Well, one of the sports medicine people took a look at the gym, Papa. You know, Tenley Albright's group. He said I shouldn't race until it heals."

"Shouldn't we do a bit more about it than that?"

"I dunno, Papa. I'll let you know after my workout."

My father placed the thick newspaper carefully on the table. I knew from the way he did it there was a major negotiation coming up.

"I would like you to come down to the bank in the morning before you go. I want you to sit in on something…according to our agreement."

"You mean the 'I get to train for the Olympics if you get to suck me into going to business school' agreement? That agreement?"

"The very one. The one that says you sit in on important meetings with me, since you are my only possible heir," said Barney dryly. He glanced over at Jeanette, who flushed. There had once been a terrible argument over the size of our family. Or should I say lack of size of our family.

"Some dull board meeting? Or an interview with the next J. P. Morgan?"

"As a matter of fact, Toni, it isn't a bank matter, it's about another of your responsibilities, the Putnam Memorial."

"Surely, Barney, you don't expect me to run the Putnam too" The sarcasm was wasted, the patriotic speech was on its way.

"It's been around two hundred years, Toni. Since your great-greats founded it."

"After killing off most of the whales in the world."

"And it's the largest of the Harvard teaching hospitals, what you students like to call the seven sisters."

"Just the pre-meds."

"There's been a Putnam on the board one way or another since the day it was founded. There's not a better hospital in the world."

"Big deal." I saw Barney flush, and realized I'd overstepped badly. Barney is not a bad guy, but he's hell on wheels when angry.

"I'm sorry, Papa," I said quickly. "What time?"

"Nine o'clock, no, a quarter to, he's coming at nine and I want you there before him."

"Who is he, Louis Pasteur?"

"His name is Aaron Scheckler."

I had to laugh. "You mean that skinny little guy who caused the riot and got tomatoes thrown all over the front of the old Putnam?"

"That's right, Toni, the research neurologist. He claims, of course, that it was the animal right's people that caused the disturbance."

"Serves him right, the jerk, crushing spines of monkeys. I met him once at a party over at the Deanery in Vanderbilt Hall. He's one creepy looking guy."

"Toni! Your language!" said my mother.

"He claims it was necessary research," continued Barney. "At any rate, he's dismissed. We have enough on him to get him out of here without a lot of nasty publicity. He's an incorrigible drunk, that's the official reason. I don't want his research brought into the discussion. You're to listen and observe. If any nosy reporter in Switzerland tries to blind-side you about this matter, you know nothing about it except what you read on your way over."

"He should be tarred and feathered," I replied, "Not politely asked to leave."

"Toni, remember, it's not about the research. As far as you're concerned, he's been offered another position elsewhere, and has accepted, and we wish him well."

"Where are you guys sending him?"

"You'll find out tomorrow, if you bother to listen."

THE FAILED SCIENTIST

Aaron Scheckler crept into Barney's office on the 30th floor of the National Farmers and Sailors Savings Bank, pausing to stare at the long bank of plate glass windows framing Boston harbor, blinking owl-like into the blazing morning sun, then twisting abruptly to face the large teak desk. A small man, quite thin, even emaciated.

He was wearing a bedraggled gray tweed jacket, tan poplin slacks, white socks and dusty penny loafers...the uniform of a Harvard research physician. He held his elbows away from his body and his hands level with his waist like some bizarre elf who was going to tackle somebody. A very large head covered with spiky black hair was awkwardly supported by his scrawny neck.

He watched my father intently as he moved, finally scuttling crab-wise into the chair in front of Barney's desk, yanking it sideways and sitting down. One baleful glance at me. His eyes gleamed from deep sockets. More than anything he reminded me of a hyena shoved into a strange cage. He did not offer to shake hands with Barney. That was a mistake. Bankers always want to shake hands before they do somebody in.

"I suppose that's a whaler," said Scheckler, staring at the model of a three masted ship in its de-humidified case in the corner of the room. He sniffed, wrinkling the bridge of a large nose. The skin stretched tight over it. Sharp ridges marked the edges as if a tent had been pitched and the ropes pulled too tight. When he talked most of the sound came from there. A florid New York accent.

"No," contradicted Barney, "A whaler would have a huge crow's nest, almost a box, up there on the mainmast." Barney leaned to one side to buzz Shirley Moyer, his secretary. "No, Dr. Scheckler, that's a trading vessel. Made a fortune sailing to and from the Spice Islands."

The doctor glared at him from across the desk, folding and unfolding his fingers in his lap as if he wanted to choke Barney. The door opened softly.

"Would you care for some coffee, or tea, perhaps?" When there was no answer, Barney nodded to Shirley and the door closed quietly.

"What really pisses me off," hissed Scheckler, "is how you people went out and slaughtered whales by the hundred thousand, to say nothing of the world's turtles." He turned to see if I was listening. "Strapped to the decks for weeks before you ate them," he continued. "For you they build skyscrapers. I sacrificed three chimpanzees to learn something about spinal cord regeneration and you run me out of town."

Barney flushed dark red along his jaw as he leaned forward. "You're leaving Dr. Scheckler, but not because of your science. We've defended a lot of unpopular science, believe me. You've been given every opportunity to discipline yourself. There have been four drunk driving arrests in six years. You no longer have a driver's license. You refused therapy, counseling, rehabilitation, whatever you want to call it. It's a record we cannot abide."

"Save that speech for the newspapers, Putnam. It's not the drinking, it was the riot. I'm an embarrassment. Now I'm excess baggage, regardless of my work. You won't admit it. When that silly Burnsides decided to go outside and face the mob of kids, and got plastered all over with tomatoes, that was my last day at Putnam."

"Dr. Burnsides was trying to help you."

"Burnsides has a martyr complex. I watched from the neurology laboratory. Did he think I was going to come down and give myself up to the mob?" Scheckler leaned forward quickly to watch Barney's reaction.

Ignoring him, Papa looked at his watch, rose up slowly and marched across the room to an antique brass telescope pointed toward the glistening harbor. He adjusted it, bent over, and peered through the eyepiece. The morning light reflected on his rough features. A rugged sea captain; even a ruthless pirate. Barney's talent for intimidation. He wanted Scheckler to see how big he was, and rough looking in spite of a two thousand dollar suit and hundred dollar tie.

"I didn't realize there were girl's dormitories down here," said Scheckler.

"I'm watching for the arrival of my daughter's Swissair flight," Barney replied. "It comes in between now and ten, then leaves at noon."

Barney motioned toward me for the first time. "I understand the two of you have met?" There was a cautious silence as Barney returned behind the massive teak desk.

"I met her once," replied Scheckler, without taking his eyes from my father. "At a cocktail party with a bunch of half-drunk medical students and Wellesley girls. Several months after she won her medal. She was very kind to me." Scheckler's turned toward me as if we were going to now have a long conversation. "Unforgettable, actually," he added.

Papa was feeling uncomfortable. Sorry he had brought up the subject. One of his strongest principles is to never discuss his family with strangers. And perhaps some guilt as he looked at the sad dark face across from him.

"Look, Dr. Scheckler," he began, "I know you've had some...unexpected legal and other expenses with all of this. Perhaps I could help out a bit, if you will let me."

Yep, I thought, Barney is feeling guilty.

"I don't need charity," snapped Scheckler. But he paused to consider. "There is Priscilla," he said slowly.

Scheckler pushed himself out of his chair and walked hesitantly over to the bank of windows. "I'm not a beggar, but I guess I would beg for Priscilla," he mumbled as he stared out over the water.

"Who's Priscilla, Doctor?" Barney's tone was wary.

Scheckler's laugh was a sharp bark. "She's my orangutan, Putnam. I understand you're shutting down the primate lab when I leave?"

Papa nodded, his face a firm mask, but I had watched Barney enough times to know when he sensed opportunity. "This Priscilla has some particular significance?" he asked quietly.

"She's everything," replied Scheckler, "She harbors the enterovirus I hope to use as the messenger for my genetic probes to re-establish myelination of the spinal nerves."

"You'll have to translate that, I'm afraid."

"In certain spinal injuries, where the spinal cord is not actually divided, there's permanent paralysis because the nerves lose their insulation, after which they're attacked by the body's own inflammatory cells and fluids. My studies hope to reverse that process before it goes too far."

"Resulting in what?"

For the first time Scheckler smiled, showing very crooked teeth. "Oh yes, Putnam, you have it there! Recovery of the lost function. The lame would walk again, as they say," he said sarcastically.

"Well, I hope you succeed, Dr. Scheckler," replied Barney smoothly.

"Putnam, if you had even the faintest hope that I was going to succeed, you would double the size of the primate lab, and you'd have some medical student drive me to work until it happened." Scheckler was fighting to control himself. "You've just made any chance of success absolutely impossible!" he snarled.

"Are you going to take the position in Athens, Dr. Scheckler?" asked my father.

"Athens, Greece, or Athens, Ohio?" replied Scheckler. His laugh was a short sarcastic bark.

"I believe we're talking about Athens, Ohio."

"Just where *is* Athens, Ohio, anyway?"

"I understand it's in the southern part of the state."

"Sounds like moonshiners and coal miners to me." said Scheckler.

"I'm certain it's a very pleasant campus. A fine university and medical school. They are looking for a neurologist."

"Have you been there?"

"Of course not."

"Then how would you know? How did you find this place anyway?"

"The Dean of the Medical School is an old classmate. William Henderson. He's a fine man," replied Barney, again showing irritation in spite of himself.

"Who did *his* dog bite?" asked Scheckler. "It's a bunch of osteopaths isn't it?"

"It's an osteopathic school of medicine. I understand a very good one."

"Oh, I bet it *is*." Scheckler turned back and walked over to Barney's desk. He put both hands down flat on the polished surface. He had very delicate hands with long thin fingers. "Priscilla's the closest thing I'm ever going to have for a wife. She's the only female primate I've encountered who doesn't mind my drinking."

"Dr. Scheckler, I will see to it that you have a great ape facility in Athens that is generously funded if that is what you wish. But this is your last chance. You're ruining yourself. If you don't care about that, I would ask that you keep yourself out of the gutter for the sake of your science. I never expect to see you again. You must not do anything to injure that animal or cause it any unreasonable pain. You should make this an opportunity at a fine new place with excellent people who need you and want you there. And I honestly wish you every success."

Barney stood up and extended his hand. Scheckler looked at him, then walked over to me. I didn't know what to do, so I stood up. I was almost a head taller than he was. He held out his hand, and I took it. His hand was very warm and soft, his grip surprisingly firm.

"I know you had nothing to do with this, Miss Putnam," he said quietly. "Don't hate me. Believe me, I feel as bad about those poor animals as any of you kids. I wish there had been another way." He pressed my hand.

"I'm very sorry, Dr. Scheckler," was all I could say. I felt really stupid.

He turned quickly away, the corner of his mouth twitching. He hustled from the room, rapping his knuckles sharply on the plate glass case where the sailing ship floated in perpetual floodlit majesty. "Athens," he snorted. "Hillbilly medicine." He slammed the door.

"That was very cruel," I said to Barney. Now I was feeling guilty.

"Actually, it was a favor, Toni. A drunk never reforms until he hits bottom."

"I take it you told your friend, Dean Henderson, that where you are sending him is your idea of 'hitting bottom'?"

Barney was watching the harbor. "Perhaps you should consider applying for the Law School, Toni. You have a nice talent for asking nasty questions."

THE HOCKEY JOCK

Swissair Flight 1172 out of Logan had a rough climb until well past Halifax. The seat-belt sign on the 747 remained on and lunch was delayed. The flight was full, a mixture of athletes and spectators all bound for Zurich, spring break, fun and games, Olympic foreplay and any other foreplay of the moment. The frustrated flight attendants gave up early and because of all of the turbulence, the bar was free.

The huge cabin was cluttered with gear that superstitious jocks would not let out of sight. Too much wine had been served, there was a lot of noise and traffic up and down the aisle.

Hughes Lawrence lurched sideways, fighting turbulence on his return from his visit to the first class section. He stumbled heavily into his seat.

"They're getting their lunch up front," he said irritably. A reflection on the fact I had made him change our seats from first to tourist.

I was reading the sports page of the Boston Globe.

"*J' accuse!*", I replied, not looking up, "Gross class discrimination against we poor *tourista!*" I finally folded the newspaper and watched his third attempt to buckle his seat belt. "One of your privileged friends up there is going to get his balls scalded if he tries having coffee."

"Harvey Thomas and Judy want us to come up to play some bridge. They'll make room for us." Lawrence sounded hopeful.

"Temporarily, I'm sure," I replied.

Huff ignored the sarcasm. "Come on, Toni, you've made your point. All the jocks back here understand you're a regular guy and all of that. Not that I've seen many paying any attention where anyone is sitting. There'll be some world class hangovers on that train tonight."

"Huff, you go. The idea of playing bridge with Judy Thomas while you and Harvey lecture us on the finer points gives me a royal pain."

"Then we'll play hearts." Lawrence still sounded hopeful.

"Huff, leave me alone!" I snapped.

He shrugged his shoulders, started to say something, finally wobbled off down the aisle. I opened the newspaper even though I'd read everything twice. I searched for the crossword puzzle. I hate crossword puzzles.

Someone sat down heavily in the aisle seat "Huff, I…" I caught myself as I turned and stared at the man in the seat beside me. He smiled, looking silly, but a good looking guy, heavy features and a swarthy complexion. Solid muscle, wearing a Harvard tee shirt and cut-offs. "Who are you?" I demanded.

"I'm the hall porter, I thought I might get your autograph." His eyes were bloodshot. The forehead, nose and chin were from an old Roman coin. It all clicked.

"I know who you are, you're Antonelli, aren't you. Hockey player, right? All-American the first year I was there?"

The smile broadened. "The same. You can call me Vincent. I have that Olympic poster of you on my wall in Vanderbilt Hall. No kidding. You can ask the guys."

"What guys?"

"Well, they're back in Boston. We'll ask them when we get back."

"At least you didn't start out with, 'where have you been all my life?'"

"I know exactly where you've been, Toni. You've been walking your poodle around Beacon Hill while I played stickball in Somerville... that's in Middlesex," he added, sounding like a tour guide.

I had to laugh.

"I hate poodles." I said, "and I don't walk around downtown. Some Italian hot-shot might bother me."

He tried to act serious, which was even worse. He ran his hand self-consciously along his temple and back along his hair.

"I've been in love with you ever since you won the bronze medal. When you were just a kid," he added emphatically.

"I thought you were in medical school."

"What's that got to do with it? I'm fourth year."

"Then what?"

"Toni, you're trying to change the subject. Are you going to go out with me? Do a little disco and stuff, or not? That's all I'm asking." Antonelli opened both hands, palms up.

"I hadn't heard you asking. Is Huff Lawrence included? He likes to dance."

"I don't dance with boys. My family will be up from Milan to watch me play. They are trying to start an Italian Olympic hockey team." He looked so dumbfounded I had to laugh. "Besides," he continued, you wouldn't be allowed to dance with anyone we don't approve...you know, Mafia stuff."

"That's bullshit, Antonelli." I had to admit he was fun.

"I was sort of hoping the front end of this airplane might fall off before Zurich. My mother is Sicilian, if she was here she would know what to do about Lawrence. She has a lot of good ideas about things like that." He paused. He seemed deep in thought. "I play hockey. We get out there and beat on each other until somebody gives up. No finesse at all." He paused again. "Nothing like what I see when you head down a slope. I'm not kidding, Toni, I've been nuts about you ever since the last games. And you won last week at Park City, yes?"

"You still have all of your teeth. Most hockey players at the Garden don't have any front teeth. Of course, I never saw the Harvards play, do they play like gentlemen?"

"Naw, these are all false. I take them out at night. I'll show you some-time if we ever get that far."

"Don't hold your breath until it happens, Vincent."

Antonelli smiled broadly. He stood up into the aisle. "They're going to serve lunch. You going out with me or not, Toni? Like I say, friends and family will be up from Italy to watch me play. You will be as safe as if you were in church with them around."

"I'm not afraid of you, Antonelli," I said. The guy amused me.

"I'll pick you up tomorrow night. The day before your first race, right? I promise to have you home and in bed…your own bed…by midnight."

"How do you know where I'm staying?"

"Don't worry, Toni, I'll find you."

NIGHT OUT

We were registered at the Davoserhof…adjoining rooms…a lawyer-like compromise between Huff's interests and my mother's sense of propriety. The Davoserhof is small and very expensive; with pretty pine paneled rooms and two of the best restaurants in Switzerland. Huff is very particular about restaurants. A small paunch protrudes gently over his belt to prove it.

I was doing my best to be pleasant. But I felt obliged to tell him about Antonelli and that I intended to go dancing. As a result of all of this Huff had been rude to the porter, which was very unusual, so he compensated by over-tipping, which was not unusual. The porter stuffed the twenty expertly in a front pocket of a threadbare black vest, thanking Huff stiffly and turned quickly toward me, hiding a knowing smile. He made a fussy show of placing my luggage in one room and Huff's in the other. He asked with studied politeness if I had any 'special needs', using the time to examine my every pore, highlight, and stitch. What his piercing brown eyes did not see, his imagination certainly supplied. That was not unusual either.

Here I was in a storybook restaurant filled with dark polished wood and a huge ceramic stove, stuffing myself with the best omelette of my life and Huff wanted to argue. We were always arguing. This one was a two-pronged argument, I wanted to go straight over to the *Weissfluhgipfel* and take it on, giving me enough time on the *Parsenn* while it was still frozen tight before the sun hit it; and he wanted to take the morning on the other side to 'warm up'. I had been told the *Parsenn* was more like a white elevator shaft than a ski run, and I wanted the best snow and the best light on it for the first time down.

The other half of the argument was less pretty. Huff began by calling it my 'night out', which, needless to say pissed me off considerably. Almost spoiled the omelette.

"Keep talking that way, Huff, and it might be a lot longer 'night out' than you might wish," I threatened.

"And I tell you he is a bullshit artist, Toni. He was fourth year when I was third. In the locker room you always heard him before you saw him. Big Italian mouth."

"Well then I guess I'll find that out, won't I, Huff?"

"C'mon, Toni. Take it easy," he pleaded. "What about your promise to decide on a formal engagement by this summer?"

"How did we get on this subject so early"

"Well?"

"That is an idea hatched by my mother and by you, Huff, and you know it! All I said was if I decided not to train for next winter I might be ready for something more…permanent. I'll tell you this, I've not made any commitment like that to you, and I'm over here to see about the Olympics, and Pearce is slinking around like he owns a piece of me. And now you! Compared to the two of you, a mouthy Italian sounds pretty good."

The *Weissfluhgipfel* was everything advertised. They had boundary poles up and a timing gate if you wanted one. To make any kind of time there was going to have to be a lot of very high speed turns. And there was a jump every hundred meters or so. That was the idea. Just the stuff for someone with legs like a telephone pole. I had Heidi Fleisch in mind. Apparently she had been there all of last week and was killing the run. I ran it twice. One thing I do is make up a lot of time with technique. When I am in the zone I carve very little and lose nothing from turning too wide. When I finished the second practice the back of my leg was biting at me like an angry snake. Huff met me at the bottom and we skied to the villages.

We wolfed down *bundnerfleisch* for a snack and then ate lunch outside…*geschnitzeltes* and *rosti*…listened to the strolling band and drank Italian wine.

Two American girls wanted my autograph. Huff turned on the urban lawyer charm which made me want to throw up. We rode the lifts to the tops of the easier slopes and skied all afternoon in brilliant sunshine.

When we came into the hotel lobby the concierge waggled a finger in my direction, looking very sly about it, and when I went over he inquired very quietly if I knew a Mr. Antonelli, and did I wish to receive a message? When I nodded, he passed me a note. I noticed he screened the entire process from Huff's line of vision, using both his desk and my body as a shield. You would have thought it contained the plans for the atom bomb. If I ever decide to be unfaithful to my husband, I think I will go live in Europe.

All the note said was, "It begins at 7:30!" What begins? Romeo and Juliet? The next millennium? The fire under the fondue? Italians are strange people.

∗   ∗   ∗

That evening I came down to the lobby at 7:30. I wore a white sheath, the upper portion was several layers, just enough of nearly transparent nylon, which covered my shoulders but left my back bare. The skirt was cream colored silk snug as skin. I piled my hair high on my head instead of the usual tight folded pigtail.

I have my mother's complexion, the best France has to offer, a delicate natural cream color which she insists I ruin with my tanned face and forearms, and there are always the different shades around my eyes and forehead which are protected by the tinted racing mask. Jeanette would prefer that I kept it all under a parasol, I suppose…so everything matches up under candlelight.

I carried a dark brown trench coat and a pair of dancing slippers and wore heavy after-ski boots. "Toni," Antonelli warned solemnly, "You'll cause a riot. My Italian cousins will stab each other over who gets to dance with you."

"I love being flattered," I said.

He looked like a kid in a candy store. I turned up a cheek for him to kiss so he could get a whiff of perfume. I was within an inch of being as tall as he was. "Where we going?" I asked. "I've never been to Davos."

"It's an Italian restaurant, half disco, half nuthouse," explained Antonelli. "About four kilometers out of town. We have several tables. It'll be stuffed with tourists, I'm afraid."

I laughed. "What do you think we are, Vincent?" I looked around the busy lobby. "I hope the Swiss are ready for this."

"All of the green stuff helps. They're used to it. Perhaps not this bad, though."

"Vincent, please leave the name of where we're going with the concierge. I promised Huff I would do that." I smiled mischievously. "I don't think Huff trusts you."

"Sounds like a good judge of character to me."

When he returned, I took his arm and we hustled out into the frigid evening air to catch a cab.

"How did the Parsenn go?" We were huddled in the back of a tiny Renault as it sped between steep banks of snow.

"Wow, what a drop! I'm OK, I've had some good runs, but a couple of those turns max out my legs. I worry about Fleisch on a run like that. She's built like a tank. I hear she takes that corner by the cliff like a bat out of hell, then muscles her way out of it as if it was nothing. There are only about four of us who can do that and stay upright. Heidi knows that. And I know her. She's planning to put the screws on." I pulled my coat tighter against the cold. The driver had the window open and was smoking a cigarette. "What about you? You guys chasing the little black puck all over the place?"

"One of the coaches said we shouldn't be on the ice. I may have to shove my stick through his ear hole tomorrow," replied Vincent.

"Sounds like fantastic team spirit!"

"We're a mess. The idea of an Italian hockey team is a joke…Jeez, Toni, don't let them know I think that. According to one of my uncles, we're going to beat the Russians, the Swedes and the Finns. What's really going to happen is everyone is going to have us for lunch. I don't even see one win. I know this sounds petty, but I think the Larrys could beat us."

"The Larrys?"

"St. Lawrence. A little college up in New York state. Play great hockey, always do. Play together. We need that. We don't have it. So, Toni, tomorrow you find out, huh?"

"Yeah. I'm not worried about that. At least I'll know where I stand. The coaches are bitching about attitude, and Pearce is hanging around whining about my condition and my leg. He keeps pressing on the hamstring and talking to himself. They all should worry. I have a year. I'll be fired up when the time comes. Half of downhill is not peaking too early. I think they have us stirred up too much. I told one of them that. They want us to start acting like the Olympics are tomorrow. Well, tomorrow I'll show them. They'll get their pound of flesh. And I'll show my rear end to Heidi Fleisch as well."

The roadhouse was noisy, packed with skiers…mostly families and mostly Italian. A huge dining area. Rustic pine and wrought iron surrounding a dance floor with the band trapped in the middle. We crowded into the tiny space reserved for us and I was swamped by children of all ages, several little girls asking shyly for my autograph. I think Vincent, in his usual habit of gross exaggeration, had oversold me considerably.

The dress code was non-existent, everything from neon-colored Parisian see-though, to jeans and a running bra. It was hot, especially in front of the huge stone fireplace. We danced in a haze of wood smoke under the peaked rafters of the blackened ceiling. Vincent Antonelli was solid as a rock to hold on to, and moved so smoothly he seemed weightless. My pulse went up more than it should have under the circumstances, and I think it showed. He pretended not to notice.

Every time we came back to the table some new specialty had been piled on my plate by another excited and voluble Italian woman who had to watch me eat it and pass judgment. I had no idea what I was eating but most of it was delicious. Wine poured freely, but I stuck with Gatorade. I knew I had my hands full tomorrow. I wasn't going to take on Hiedi Fleish with a hangover.

Toward the end of the evening, when many of the families were gathering to leave, a slender boy walked toward our table from across the nearly empty dance floor. He was about four inches shorter than I am. He was darkly handsome, even so young, with jet black hair, pale skin and smooth cheeks. Early in his teens. He held his head high as he approached. He watched me with solemn eyes separated by a hawk-like narrow nose. Even short and thin and young, he looked dangerous. He glanced meaningfully at Vincent, who smiled at him and nodded, whereupon the boy turned and asked me to dance! I'm sure my jaw dropped, but I caught myself and glanced at Vincent. He raised his eyebrows slightly. Enough to tell me I was on my own.

That was not a problem. I was not about to embarrass a polite handsome man, even if he was only fourteen. I stood up slowly and took his arm, and he led me out onto the floor. I heard a very primitive folk song. The boy danced exquisitely. His face was radiant, especially when he shot glances toward the table from which he had approached me.

When the music stopped we were both sweating. My heart was pounding, this time from the exercise. There were cheers from several tables mixed with some phrases that sounded earthy to me. He marched me back to Vincent's table, bowed solemnly to both of us and left. After I was seated, Vincent leaned over.

"You know what that was all about?" he asked.

"Hardly, but it was fun," I replied.

"What happened, I'm sure, Toni, is the boy made some sort of remark about you while he was watching from his table, and his brothers and cousins started to bait him, and had him over a barrel daring him that he was afraid to make a move on you. If you had belittled him he would have never been allowed to forget it. What you did and the way you did it shows a very kind heart, Toni Putnam." Vincent looked me up and down as if he was seeing me for the first time. "You're quite a woman," he said quietly.

I realized as I watched those teasing brown eyes that I was falling in love with Vincent Antonelli. It was happening and there was nothing I could do about it. When he helped me into my trench coat, his hands passed over my shoulders and I found myself fantasizing what it would feel like if he was sliding off the gauzy straps from my shoulders instead of hustling me into that ugly coat. I wanted to turn around and put my arms around his neck and hold him forever. The bug bit me then and there. It bit me hard. I fought for control before I made a fool of myself.

RACE DAY

It was Race Day. Fourteen skiers, all the others well known to me, all older; I'd been the ski prodigy, it had made for a lot on newspaper ink. But up here with the wind whipping ice crystals through the early morning sunshine it meant nothing.

Yesterday's warm weather created hard crusted surface ice, exactly how much and where was up to us to find out. If what looked like hard packed snow at the outer edge of the course turned out to be hard-pan ice, the price would be sliding on your ass for sixty feet, or worse, a broken leg.

There was not much of a crowd, too much fun the night before. As for TV coverage, we were told we were running a distant second to a spring-break wet tee shirt contest in Fort Lauderdale. The timer was a diffident Swiss, a shapeless mass bundled against the frigid wind with only a sharp pointed nose sticking out of a fur-lined parka, eyes glaring over a frosted moustache, looking like an angry mole. He had no doubt loaded up on early morning schnapps for anti-freeze, and kept forgetting to re-set the timer. As a result some of the readings at the bottom were screwed up.

Pearce was up there, fussing around Cathy Newell and myself, the only two Americans. He wasn't wearing a hat, seemed oblivious to the wind-blown wisps of blond hair back and forth across his face. I was having trouble keeping warm, but I was certain if I went into the warming hut he would follow me in and demand to have me show him the back of my leg. He looked pained when I told him there was no bruise there; I was lying and he knew it. There was a stripe of purple from my butt halfway to my knee.

I was ninth out of the gate, heaving myself well out over the tips and picked up a lot of speed before the first jump. At the turn at the cliff I had a moment of panic, but the edges caught in plenty of time and I shot out of it and into a monster jump with good balance. I made a mental note it was the essential move of this run…high speed going into that jump was going to be the difference for sure, barring something going wrong. I had excellent control the entire run, didn't touch a flag, and the ice was breaking up enough that I could edge perfectly. I couldn't believe at the bottom that I was in second place behind Heidi Fleish.

The crowd had grown at the bottom, but were huddled like groups of musk oxen against the sudden fury of the wind and ice. The sun had disappeared and visibility dropped with each windy gust. Huff was just beyond the rope, his parka covered with sleet. I skied over and hugged him and we studied the times on the lighted board.

"Toni, you're favoring that leg, you realize that?" he demanded. I ignored him. My time was recorded as .4 seconds slower than Heidi which was a laugh under these conditions. Huff's heavy mitten gripped my chin, turning me toward him. I jerked away. "Toni, let it go. This race doesn't mean anything except some column in the back of the sport's pages. Let it go!"

I watched Heidi Fleisch and her husband moving in a clot of well-wishers toward a chalet. "She isn't even going to take a second run," I said, "It's scheduled to be the best out of two." I couldn't believe she would be so cock-sure as to walk away.

"Toni, nobody is going to take another run in these conditions, I'll bet the course will be closed before you could get back up there."

The two skiers racing after me were down, their times were terrible. A yellow light came on the board…someone had fallen up there. I looked across the finish area and saw Vincent standing in the crowd, bareheaded and blowing into his cupped hands as he watched me.

"I have another run coming," I insisted.

"So does everybody," replied Huff. "What good would that do? Are you nuts or something? What's got into you Toni?" He followed my eyes. When he saw I was looking at Vincent, his face froze. He gripped the sleeve of my parka. "Come on, Toni, we're getting out of here. This isn't the Olympics and it wouldn't make any difference if it was."

I tore my arm away, picked up my skis and headed for the lift.

Pearce was waiting at the top. It was obvious from his expression that Huff had called ahead. Pearce was now wearing a bright green helmet which made him look like a large frosted elf. He held up his hand like a traffic cop, which was even sillier.

"No Toni," he insisted, "you're not going. You belong in a hot tub." He danced around me as I snapped on the skis. "Toni," he pleaded, "don't do this. Huff Lawrence said you were favoring the leg. Don't do this!" He did his ridiculous little dance again. I think he was working up the nerve to tackle me.

I slid over to the man huddled beside the timing gate. He glared at me, exhaling frosty air smelling of peppermint schnapps. I yanked my thumb at him to turn the damn thing on and jumped behind the gate.

I shot straight down the fall line. The thick freshly driven snow covered all ruts and was fast as white lightening. By the second turn it felt faster than any of the practices yesterday or the first run today and I knew I could get the half second I needed on Fleisch. I let them run flat out.

I screeched into the turn at the cliff but when I strained to go airborne my left leg gave out. A wave of shocking pain shot to my brain
and the leg went limp. In a split second my weight shifted too far back
and the inner edges failed to bite. I drifted right at tremendous speed
and realized the only chance to stay on the course was to attempt to
jump with my right leg. I gave it everything I had at the lip of the
jump. Suddenly I was ten feet above the snow, with the hill falling
away, but to my horror was far to the right side of the course. I clipped
the top of a small pine tree and somersaulted. I saw the sky spin above
me, hit a glancing blow on an edge of granite and careened over the
cliff. There was a crashing sound as I struck more pine branches,
another split second of free fall, then I smashed on the rocks below.
My helmet and my back hit at the same moment. The blow to the
head sent a bright yellow flash behind my eyes. As my back struck, a
terrible electric shock flashed down both legs and seemed to burn like
fire on the soles of my feet. Then the pain stopped. Everything turned
dark brown, then silent blackness.

PARALYSIS

The boy leaned over me. Cheeks smooth as hard brown marble, dark blue eyes, young, worried. He rubbed one of my hands and then the other vigorously between his own. He was speaking to me but I couldn't hear him. A brown mist thickened and he faded into it. I called out for him.

I felt a throbbing noise growing louder, finally shaking the earth. The boy came back into focus. He held my head firmly and leaned very close. He said something to someone in German. The throbbing noise swept away his voice, snow swirled, a helicopter swung back and forth above us. Three men in bright orange coveralls jumped into the snow before it settled and shoved the boy aside. They stood over me, the driving snow quickly coating their coveralls. A stocky man standing at my feet waved his arm in the wind, swinging it in a circle...gesturing not to stop the rotor. Then he pointed at me and a second rescuer knelt at my head.

"We're taking you to Chur," he shouted in crisp English. There's a fine orthopedic center there." When I moved he put a firm hand on my chest. "Don't move," he commanded, not sounding nearly as polite.

A wire basket with a board floor crunched down beside me. Sandbags squeezed both sides of my head and a strap tightened over my forehead. I swayed crazily in the air as I was lifted to the helicopter and bounced inside like a piece of luggage. It was then that I realized there was no pain except where the strap pressed on my forehead. There was no pain at all in my legs. I started screaming. I was still screaming as the thumping of the motor increased and we lifted over the mountains. All I could see out of the open door was blinding snow. Someone slammed it shut. Loud worried German voices drifted back from the front. I stopped screaming and started sobbing. The boss-man appeared over me and gently wiped the tears aside with a small gauze sponge.

*   *   *

"I am Dr. Kostner," the surgeon said. "Miss Putnam, you need a spinal exploration. We call it a laminectomy."

It was well past midnight. It seemed more like five years. My useless legs had been spread apart and a catheter inserted to drain urine, the nurse started to lift my legs out of the stirrups, but two stony-faced young doctors ordered her away and started poking something. I could see their shadows with the light behind them, they would do something, then look at each other and shake their heads and then do it again. When I asked them what they were doing the younger one appeared over the sheet between my knees and announced importantly that they were testing for 'anal wink'. That was all. I asked again and he only shrugged as if he suddenly no longer understood English. I was paralyzed, and they were interested in whether my anal…whatever that was…winked or not? It seemed to me that deserved some explanation.

There had been a CT scan, and thirty minutes later an MRI. All sorts of X-rays. All with my back kept completely rigid. Blood was drawn. A woman about forty years old with prematurely gray hair spent thirty minutes sticking pins in me and asking with a thick accent if I felt them.

I asked her about the 'anal wink.' She smiled and said, "sacral sparing would mean you have only an incomplete cord injury."

"Well?"

Her face fell. "I'm sorry, there's no response," she said.

Kostner cut into my mind-wandering. I'd forgotten he was trying to talk to me. I suppose it was the narcotics.

"I've spoken at length with your father, Miss Putnam, and with several of the neurosurgeons at the Putnam."

I will give Kostner credit, he made no attempt to hide the fact that he was under a lot of pressure. "The studies show us a very unusual injury. You landed on a jagged rock which crushed the dorsal lamina of the last thoracic vertebra. The cord has not been transected…cut in two. But it has been badly bruised, and there are bone fragments against it. We…the Putnam doctors and I…have decided there should be an immediate exploration to be certain there isn't bleeding, or pressure, or even further injury if you move. You've had only a very minor brain concussion. Your racing helmet saved you."

Saved me for what, I wondered. "Am I going to get better?"

"I…cannot say."

"Will you know after you do the surgery?"

"I don't think we will. It's going to be a matter of time."

"How much time?"

"If you're going to recover there should be signs in two weeks."

"I'd like to talk to Mr. Lawrence if I may."

"Certainly. He's right outside."

"And let's get this over with."

"We will proceed within the hour, Miss Putnam." Kostner hurried out of the room.

Hughes Lawrence was haggard, deep lines in his cheeks, eyes bloodshot, lips tightly compressed. His hands shook and the fingers were icy as he took mine.

"My God, Toni," was all he could say.

"Huff, I want out of here the very first moment possible, you hear me?" I demanded.

"Barney says the same, Toni. Kostner told him they would arrange to clear out the upper cabin of a 747 tomorrow, and if the surgery is as he expects, he saw no reason you couldn't be on your way home tomorrow. We're making those arrangements."

"Where's Vincent Antonelli? Is he around?" I asked.

"How would I know? Who cares!"

"Is he around?" I repeated.

"He's been here since you landed. He's been a big pain in the ass. Demanded to see all of the scans, X-rays, everything. He's only a medical student. Kostner should have thrown him out!"

"I want to see him."

"Toni, he really has no business…I don't think Barney…"

"Quit acting like an idiot, Huff, and send Antonelli in here."

Antonelli needed a shave. Other than that he looked pretty good. What surprised me was how important he had become to me. I wanted for him to stand there so I could look at him.

"Pretty nasty spill, I hear," he said.

"I'm finished," I replied. I had a big lump in my throat. There wasn't going to be any tomorrow. Not with Vincent Antonelli. It was over before it started.

"I'm paraplegic, Vince, no legs. Dead from the belly down."

"No way," replied Antonelli. "I looked at all the stuff. You're going to be fine."

"Kostner isn't making those sort of promises."

"What's he know? Antonelli says full recovery."

"Spoken like a non-combatant," I said nastily.

Antonelli acted as if he didn't hear.

"Seriously, Toni, I hear this guy is really good. I'm on the phone to the Putnam after Kostner talked to them. They know him, said he is really good. I even talked to your father."

Antonelli had been busy. "How's Barney taking this?"

"He's scared, Toni, who wouldn't be? I promised him I wouldn't let you out of my sight until you were in a bed in the Putnam. I told him there was just a bad bruise and that you were going to be fine."

I had to laugh. "You better be right or Barney will flush you down the nearest toilet and I'm going to help him."

Antonelli leaned over the bed and kissed me gently on the forehead. "You're my girl, remember?" he asked. "And I'm promising you that you're going to be fine. Antonelli is never wrong." He sensed how much I needed him and slid his arms under my shoulders and hugged me. He smelled like garlic and he needed a shower. His beard stubble was rough against my cheek. I didn't want him to ever let me go.

THE RAG DOLL

The upper deck of the Swissair 747 had been cleared, hung with white pull drapes and my bed fastened in the center. Huff and Vincent had seats just beyond the drapes. I was hardly awake from the surgery before the transfer began. Kostner spent ten minutes with me, looking tired but relieved. He described what he called a 'decompression' as routine, no blood clot, no further bleeding, no actual division of the spinal cord; several bone fragments were removed and the whole thing 'stabilized', whatever that meant. I was free to fly away!

So now we were airborne. There had been a minimum of airport hassle although getting me up the front steps was a circus. I was strapped in and helpless while they did the acrobatics only this time I was wide awake. There was some pain from the incision on my back which I welcomed because there was no feeling below that. The catheter in my bladder tore away from the bag while they were carrying me and sprinkled urine over the flight crew who were watching. That started a wave of gloom sweeping over me. It didn't help that both Huff and Vince looked like they were going to a funeral...or perhaps that was only my imagination. A flight attendant tried to get me to drink some orange juice and I felt like throwing it at her. She pulled the drape and left me alone.

That only increased the feeling of total helplessness.

For the first time in my life I wanted to die. I wondered if I just set my mind to it, and thought hard enough, I could make my heart stop and make everything go away forever. I heard the metal scrape of the drape and turned my head to see Antonelli looking at me.

"You don't look too happy, Toni." He spoke very softly.

I could feel tears running down the side of my face. "I want out of life, Antonelli," I said. "I can't live as a cripple. I know I can't." I started sobbing.

He turned around and closed the drape behind him. Then he came over and dabbed at my face with his handkerchief. He had shaved and wore a well pressed two button jacket, but looked like he hadn't slept for two days. Two days, I thought. Seems like a lifetime. I had been getting ready to go dancing.

"You clean up pretty good, Antonelli," I said lamely. No more dancing for me.

"You know, Toni, that's exactly what you need," he said.

"Go dancing, Vince? That's hardly funny."

"I mean one of my world-famous warm sponge baths. A great picker-upper for a maiden in distress."

"Is this your routine for the second date?" I asked. He had me smiling again.

But he had disappeared. After a muted conversation and some metallic clinking he re-appeared with a stainless steel bowl of steaming water in which floated a small bar of soap. A towel and several face-cloths were draped over his shoulders.

He wore a phony professional look on his face.

"You should've been a hair-dresser," I said.

Very carefully he reached behind my neck and pulled the tie on the hospital gown, then slid it down. I felt him deftly covering my breasts with the wash-cloths just before he got to the nipples. He started to bathe one arm slowly and solemnly. I let him do all of the work. It felt wonderful

I hadn't had a decent bath since the morning before the accident. Although I was having fun watching his face, I made myself close my eyes and let him do anything he wanted. When he arrived at the armpit with its thick tuft of black hair, he scrubbed very carefully and thoroughly. "Very Sicilian," was all he said.

He did the other arm, then my chest, then started to scrub over my stomach but a horror filled me when I couldn't feel him more than halfway down my abdomen. He sensed this.

"We'll save the rest for the third date,' he announced, pulling up the gown.

He was tying the gown behind my neck when the drapes snapped open and Huff stood staring at us. His face flushed beet red.

"What the hell is going on in here!" he demanded. He reached for Vincent, shaking him roughly, spilling half of the water in the bowl.

"Stop it!" I shouted.

The startled flight attendant appeared and snatched away the bowl. The two men looked like angry curs. It sickened me.

"Are you going to fight over *me*? *Me*? A rag doll? What use could I ever be to either of you? Get out of here both of you. Leave me alone!" The uncontrollable sobbing returned.

The young flight attendant hurried in with two sleeping pills. Her hand shook as she steadied my chin and rolled the pills into my mouth from a small paper cup. Then she supplied a glass of water and bent a flexible straw to my lips so I could choke them down. Tears brimmed over her lower lids and she turned her face away trying to hide them. The side of her neck beneath a tight blonde bun was deeply tanned. Mountain tan. High thin air and the hiss of skis running hard. I knew where she had been and where I could never go again. I concentrated on the ceiling of the droning airplane and finally drifted off to sleep.

* * *

I woke up as we started to descend. It must have been a slight change in engine pitch, or perhaps the change in pressure. Huff was standing between the parted drapes. I think he had been there for some time. I could see Vincent Antonelli over by the far window. It was late afternoon. "Come in, Huff, and close the drapes," I said.

He came up beside my bed looking like a whipped Labrador.

"Toni, I'm so sorry," he said. I put my finger up to his lips.

"Don't, Huff," I said. "Don't apologize. You haven't done anything wrong."

He seemed to relax. "Huff, you are a really sweet guy," I continued, "and I've been doing a lot of thinking. This isn't working." He started to object but I stopped him.

"Huff, I know if this doesn't…you know…work out with my legs, that you would stick with me. I know you love me. Knowing you, the man that you are, you would stay with me even if you stopped loving me. You're a fine wonderful man and I've tried very hard to love you. But I don't. It's my fault, nothing you've ever done. I want you to go find someone who is going to treat you decently…as you deserve to be treated."

He wanted to say something, but I put my finger to my lips. "There's more to it than that, Huff, I want to be free. Especially now…after this. Sometimes I hate myself when I act the way I do. And particularly now, I don't think I can handle that."

"Toni, don't talk like this. You just need some time."

"Then give it to me, Huff."

He stood looking at me. Deep sad lines grooved his cheeks.

"What can I do, Toni?" he begged. "I can't give you up. I love you, I always have…ever since we were kids…down at Nantucket…I think I always will."

"I know you have, Huff. You have always been wonderful to me. It's way past time for you to love somebody else. Huff, darling, this would have happened anyway. And it would have been a lot worse for both of us. Don't wait for me. It's over."

I stared again at the ceiling. After a long pause I heard the drapes slither as he closed them and turned away.

DENIAL

"I'm Winfield Reynolds, Miss Putnam," announced the surgeon.

How well I knew. Winfield Reynolds II, Chief of Neurosurgery at the Putnam. He managed to say the same thing every time he came into my room leading his preppie parade. Like my mind was addled and I had forgotten who he was. Hardly. Not that frozen superior expression plastered over a milky face topped by carefully combed long strands of hair sliding off of his bald spot. When he bent over me with all of his self-important fussy little tests, his pink bald spot reminded me of the rear end of a jackass.

He always walked like he was late for a subway train, practically screeching to a stop at my bedside, the rest of the entourage flowing around the bed, expecting to see a miracle, no doubt. It included a self-important chief resident, several inferior residents, I assumed from the hang-dog looks, and a bored medical student who always sidled over to perch on the windowsill where he stared far down at the entryway to the Putnam.

Reynolds cleared his throat when he saw I wasn't paying any attention. I gave him a look that should have turned him to stone, which he rewarded with a wintery smile beneath his trim white moustache. "I asked how you were feeling?" he repeated politely.

The head nurse arrived late, looking flustered, pushing a squeaky rack of charts up to the bedside. Reynolds glared at her. The nurse looked steadily at me, ignoring him, and from her expression I understood why the French peasantry had guillotined the aristocrats.

"How are you feeling today?" repeated Reynolds, apparently for the third time. His voice squeaked as he tried to hide his irritation.

"Compared to what?" I replied nastily. I didn't care.

Without answering he turned back the sheet covering my legs. I felt the gown slide along my belly where the feeling started, I'm sure he was adjusting it so everything was prim and proper...I didn't give a damn about that either. He fiddled around with a small rubber hammer and stuck some pins in somewhere. He shrugged his shoulders, turning to the chief resident, "You get anything?" he asked.

The resident shook his head 'no'. Reynolds pulled up the sheet.

"Do you have any questions for us?" asked Reynolds. Apparently the show was over.

"When am I walking out of here?" I asked.

There was a long pause. The medical student was finally interested.

"I think you should shift your focus," replied Reynolds carefully. "I'm not getting very good reports from physical medicine, Toni. You must start to pull yourself out of this. Your incision is perfectly healed. I told you on my last visit how important physical therapy and re-hab is going to be in all of this."

"Why do you ask me for questions, *Winnie*, and then answer me with bullshit when I ask one?"

I heard Winfield Reynold's sharp intake of breath. It was very quiet in the room.

"I...apologize Miss Putnam, for taking any liberty with your first name," he said stiffly. "I meant no insult."

"Leave me alone!" I snapped. I was fighting back tears. I was damned if I was going to cry in front of that medical student.

The wheels of the cart squealed on the tile floor as the parade left. Out in the hallway I heard Reynolds braying at length about psychic trauma, failure of acceptance and other assorted crimes of the paralytic. Followed by a long period of mumbling, and then the cart squealed off and there was silence except for the soap opera on a television across the hall.

Twenty minutes later the head nurse came in. She pressed the button on the console by my pillow and the bed hummed down to the lowered position. She sat down beside me and took my hand in both of hers, holding it up to her face. Her hands were warm, slightly rough, and her cheek was very smooth. I'll bet she had a flock of kids over in Roxbury or somewhere.

"You got the nut-case assignment, huh?" I asked.

She laughed. "Right. Something like that."

"I'll apologize to Reynolds. But tell him never to bring that snotty student back in here."

"No need to apologize, Toni, he understands. We all do. We have some idea how you feel." She paused.

"Reynolds is really a good guy even if he does walk around most of the time like he has a cob up his ass," she added.

We both laughed. I felt better.

She squeezed my hand slightly. "You have to get out of this rut. This rage. There has to be someone. Do you have a minister?"

"I'm not religious."

"We have…you know…our own people."

"You think I need a shrink? I really am a nut-case? Am I that far gone?"

She opened my bedside table and took out my comb. She pushed my chin away and scooped out the mass of hair from behind my head. She turned my chin back and started to comb slowly, making long slow gentle strokes from my forehead down to the ends where she stopped to untangle them. "That's two questions, Toni. Yes, you could get some help from a psychiatrist. After today, Reynolds will request one anyway. He always does that after he gets cussed out. And the second part is 'no', you're not that far gone, just perhaps a little ahead of schedule."

"You mean I'm not the only bitch in the place?"

She smiled at me sadly. "Toni, it's almost routine. It's to be expected. At least at some point. Everybody around here knows they're dealing with high voltage. Some of the paraplegics actually do physical things. The important thing is to get through it. Get over it. Otherwise you'll have no happy days left in your life." She said no more, finished combing, replaced the comb, and left.

*   *   *

It was in the physical therapy pool where I met up with Vince Antonelli. Fourteen days since the accident, twelve days back in the Putnam. I had heard he was a real nuisance all over the hospital, getting out my reports…and there was a ton of them, electro-myograms, repeat MRI's, the opinions of four or five neurologists, kidney specialists, you name it. The nurses all knew Antonelli and took turns teasing him. A night nurse told me he fell asleep two nights ago at the nursing station with his head on his folded arms and my chart pinned underneath. Wouldn't let them have it.

Here he was, big as life, walking along the side of the tiled pool in the foggy heat looking for me. I was floating with my arms around the neck of a huge black man named George while he made my legs float back and forth in the steaming water. Antonelli was solid muscle, I don't know if it was hockey, or weights or both, but it all fit and rippled, and he knew it. He jumped in and waded over to us.

"Hi," he said, sounding like he came there every day.

"What are you doing here?" I asked.

"I asked the Dean if I could finish up with a physical therapy elective instead of doing infectious disease over at the City. He allowed as how since there were only ten days left, and I was a long way from any possible special honors; he, in effect, could care less where I spent my time. A really nice guy. I always did think so."

"They're going to be glad to get rid of you up on the Quadrangle, Vince," I laughed.

"So," said Vincent, looking hopefully at George, who weighed more than both of us put together, "if I could have my patient, I'll get to work."

George handed me over gently. "You be mighty careful, doctor, or George will come back over and drown you. This is my special lady."

"Thank you, George," I said and gave him a final squeeze.

Vincent had something other than physical therapy on his mind. He wrapped his arms around my chest from behind, and towed me over to a far corner. George watched steadily from across the pool.

"Toni, there's something going on that you need to know. It's driving me screwy, but I have to talk to you about it," Vincent said. His face was beside my ear.

"If it's anything about you and Huff, I don't want to hear it."

"No, no," he objected, "much more important than that. Do you get the same vibes that I do, that everyone around here thinks it's all over as far as recovery of your legs is concerned?"

That hit hard. "Vincent, turn me around so I can see your face," I demanded. He turned me in the water and we faced each other, his hand holding me gently afloat. "What do *you* hear?" I demanded.

"Just what you think. They're calling it a 'contusion injury'. The nerves going to the legs from the injured spinal cord are all there, but are losing their insulation, what's called myelin. And when it's gone, so is any chance of recovery of walking."

I had never seen him look so serious. "I guess that's what all the wheelchair training and 'let's get on with it' is all about?"

"Yeah."

"And Barney's going on about this special Dodge van that George is going to teach me to drive when it gets here?"

"Right, Toni."

"Well, so what are you? The one who's supposed to break the bad news?" I felt a rising sense of panic.

"Toni, there's somebody who thinks he can get you well. I've talked to him."

"*What! Who?*"

"Aaron Scheckler. I talked to him," he repeated.

"My God! He's in Ohio! Barney ran him off. I was there when he did it."

"The same. We talked about that…he's pretty bitter, wouldn't listen at first, but I kept him on the line. Then he started asking questions. Asked a whole bunch of questions. It's a wonder I'm not in jail, the stuff I dragged out from around here."

Vince swung me around so our faces were against each other. His beard was rough.

"He says you have a shot, but have to act quickly."

Vincent signaled George to come get me. "Nobody around here's going to like this idea at all," Vincent said quietly. "Especially your father."

I felt an enormous surge of hope as Vincent passed me back to George. "Get up to my room tonight. We have to talk," I said.

I hugged George as tight as I could. "Come on, big man, let's get these flippers loosened up!"

A Thread of Hope

Antonelli crept in after midnight. He wore a medical student I.D, a blood-splattered white lab coat over an open-collar oxford shirt, mussed poplin trousers, and penny loafers. The Harvard medical student uniform.

"Vince, what's going on?," I asked.

"Well, after Scheckler left your father's building on the day we caught the flight to Zurich, he bought a beat-up old van, packed up his books, cleaned out all of his files on the lab computer, and took off with that ape in the van…"

"It's a orangutan, not an ape…"

"Orangutan…ape, whatever. Can you imagine Scheckler roaring down the freeways without a driver's license with that ape peering out the back window?"

"How do you know this?'

"I hang around the neurology lab. Once anyone sees the I.D., you might as well be a piece of glassware. I heard plenty. Mostly, the people up there say Scheckler was the best cell biologist ever to set foot in that lab. Several of them say he was on to something. They were plenty sorry to see him leave."

"You better explain," I said. I felt uneasy. I'm not into hero worship.

"Toni, I'm not the hottest student there ever was in cell biology, but I've done nothing else for the past week. It's one hell of a dose to swallow."

"Lead on, Antonelli, I want to hear it all."

"Well, it starts with your anti-MAG study, and the ELISA titer."

"I'm lost already."

"Be patient. It gets worse. ELISA stands for enzyme-linked-immunoabsorbant assay. It happens when you're losing myelin...the stuff that insulates spinal nerves so they can conduct electricity. Your's is off the chart. You're within a few weeks of being beyond any possibility of repair."

I felt a nauseating cramp like I was having diarrhea. For all I knew, I *was* having diarrhea.

"You told me about that in the pool, Vince. I don't have to hear it again."

I smelled carefully. No diarrhea. "What's Scheckler have to do with this?"

"He's taken the myelin repair gene from a human and spliced it into a polio virus. He intends to use the virus as a messenger to get the gene into the cells in the spinal cord that will then cause those cells to quit screwing off and repair the damage."

"You mean polio virus like in infantile paralysis?"

"Yeah, but you've been immunized for that, right?"

"Sure, so has every two-year-old. "So where's he get this special virus? Polio only lives in primates. It can't be kept alive in anything else."

Vincent looked impressed. "You were awake in freshman biology a lot longer than I was."

"So?"

"So that's where Priscilla comes in. You know, the ape...or orang-utan...or whatever. Priscilla is the carrier of the virus. Scheckler claims he can depress Priscilla's immune system with a drug, four hours later she gets a cold and the sniffles, and the virus pours out in the mucus.

Mix up a little in some grapefruit juice, and presto! the virus is in the gut and headed for the nervous system. Just like old times with Franklin Roosevelt in his wheelchair and all of that. Only this time the virus is working for you. It gets knocked off before it hurts you."

"Drink ape snot? I would rather be paralyzed."

"Toni, don't say that...even kidding. Besides it's orangutan snot."

"And then what?" There had been diarrhea...I could smell it. I pushed Vincent away, hoping he couldn't...yet. My colon was as bad as my legs. I couldn't feel anything and it had a mind of its own.

"What happens next, Toni, is the messenger virus gets into the repair cells, the repair gets turned on, the patient's immune system gets the idea the virus is around, the killer T cells kill the virus, and all the patient has is some fever and a headache. Several days later the nerves start to work. All's said and done except for the Nobel Prize." Vincent sniffed the air, started to say something, realized what had happened, clenched his jaw and said nothing.

"And people here believe that?"

"They sure do. Not everybody. There are those who say it's the chance of a lifetime, but there are others who say Scheckler can't stay sober long enough to eat lunch, let alone splice up a virus. Martin, the chief neurosurgery resident, is trying to pull Scheckler's stuff back up from the hard disk of the lab computer. He's going to get fired if anybody finds out about that."

The night nurse came in, placed some sleeping pills and a paper cup of water on the bedside table, and looked Antonelli over closely.

"I'll be back as soon as I finish meds, Miss Putnam," she said significantly. Good nose, I thought.

"And you talked to Scheckler?" I asked. I knew that. I was fighting to get control of myself. I had to make a decision. It had to be the right decision.

"Yep, a bunch of times."

"Was he interested in me? In my case?"

"He was wary. Like I say, he asked a lot of questions. Every time I called back with more stuff he was more interested."

"Has this worked? Has he helped anybody?"

"No. He has a Phase I trial permit from the National Institutes of Health. That's small numbers of patients tested for safety and efficacy. He can try it on four or five subjects, maximum. Nobody knows anything for sure. There's a rumor he tried it on one person down there...a young guy who was paralyzed from the neck down from a motorcycle wreck, and all the guy got was diarrhea for three days."

Vincent looked uncomfortable. "But that's just a rumor," he repeated.

"I could handle the diarrhea, or pain, or whatever. I'm not sure I could handle the disappointment," I said.

Vincent handed me the cup and the two pills. "You better decide quick, Toni," he said. "Scheckler says if you're not there by next weekend, forget it."

"Would you do it Vincent? Take an altered polio bug? From Scheckler?"

"Damn right I would."

I tossed down the sleeping pills. "Ask the nurse to come in and clean me up, Vince." He leaned down over me and kissed me hard.

"We're going to get through this, Toni," he said.

I was trying not to let go and start crying or screaming. I was scared and I was ashamed of the way I smelled, and I couldn't do anything about either one except hang on to Vince like I was drowning.

Half an hour later he was still pacing in the hallway after the nurse had cleaned me up and opened the window drapes. I felt myself going. Scheckler's face shimmered on the ceiling.

AT THE EDGE OF MADNESS

I knew the next morning that this day was the dividing point of my life. I knew it. It had been a restless night, but the most wonderful thing about it was I dreamed I was back on the top of a snowy mountain with the wind screaming across the top of the slope. My hair blew around my face, ice crystals stung my cheeks and I vaulted myself into the thin air. The slope fell away, the skis scraped sharply just as they had a thousand times, I streaked into a turn, feeling my body sag down against the G forces, then my legs catapulted me back into the air, every breath so cold my throat burned. I begged the darkness to send me into that cold sunlight forever.

I awakened with a start to find it was still the middle of the night and the urine bag had overfilled and was leaking. Also I was sweating like a pig and probably smelled like one. I cried until I fell back asleep. Then it was morning.

The morning routine on the ward was to 'progress'. Get through the dependency trip. Recover. Become a *person*, not a *cripple*. A steady stream of care-givers, from Winfield Reynolds II all the way down to my physical therapy buddy, George, delivered the same message. Well, screw them. I wanted my legs back.

Therefore, I was a 'problem'. I had *failed to accept the injury*. The catechism of this particular religion was depression: anger: and denial; *'everyone goes through this'*, I was repeatedly lectured, so the idea was to get through it and get on with a new life.

Screw them all. I wanted my legs back. There was Reynolds, and the head nurse…as sweet as she was…two physical medicine residents, who showed me everything from jelly-filled whoopee bags to prevent pressure sores, automatic lifts for bedroom, bath and automobile; rectal suppositories and enema kits; body creams, uplifting literature, chat groups on the internet, and a preacher who quickly left, I think embarrassed by my language. There was a shrink who was a nice guy and came the closest to making me listen except that I remembered that he was a 440 track champ at Harvard when I was in grade school and still obviously had his own solid set of legs. So I threw him out too.

What it amounted to was that I was down to George. He had been in the unit even before the Vietnam War when the Putnam had entered physical rehabilitation in a serious and well-funded way. George always was the one who was there when the hard hits were coming. George was the one who came into my room with the wheelchair a week ago. Nothing I had ever seen horrified me like that wheelchair did. It might as well have been an electric chair.

"Now, Miss Putnam," George said in that silky-soft voice, "If you want me to carry you from place to place for the rest of your life, you just say the word and old George will do that. Otherwise you have to get that handsome ass of yours into this chair. It's this chair or old George, nobody else gets to carry you but me or this chair." He was so serious I had to laugh. I knew it was an act. I know he had done that for a thousand others.

"George, I know you say that to all the girls," I replied.

"I wouldn't dare to talk to most other girls the way I talk to you, Miss Putnam. You're my special lady." If George was married, there is some very lucky woman out there.

So there was a *convergence*, as the astrologers say, things were coming in a rush that I had no control over. I was well enough that I was to be discharged. The special van that Barney had purchased and equipped was waiting in the parking lot and George was assigned to teach me to drive it and to keep at it until I had the special license. And time was running out as far as Aaron Scheckler was concerned. So George was my designated hitter.

After the morning in the pool I ate my final lunch in the Wendy's in the mock-up where they teach paraplegics everything from wheelchair ATM procedure…"don't do it if there's anyone else around…your chance of getting mugged is still excessive, but don't carry cash out on the street either,"…to how to clean up after your dog…even if you don't have a dog…a special little do-dad. *That* physical therapist was a honey-blonde with china-blue eyes, a knock-out figure, and legs that would have stopped a funeral procession. She called the 'problem' she was teaching, "How to deal with dog do-do." Wonderful stuff like that.

I met George in the parking lot where he was loading my belongings in the back of the new van. He inserted a key by the side entrance, the door slid back and a grating emerged. It slowly whirred to the ground.

"Go on," he said simply, handing me a remote. I wheeled and whirred myself inside. He clicked me into position behind the wheel, showed me the controls for the accelerator and brake and turned the key in the ignition.

If he was ever worried as we went through afternoon Boston traffic along Storrow Drive he gave no indication. I managed to stall the thing in the middle of Copley Square. He totally ignored the swearing, honking and fist-shaking. But I had the definite feeling if anyone had jumped out to yell in my face he would have pinched their head off. We stopped very briefly at police headquarters, George went inside for no more than ten minutes and when he returned he threw the special license on the dash.

"The cops say you are one fine handicapped driver," he explained simply.

We ended up in front of my home on Louisburg Square. He started to get out the passenger door. I pulled him over to me and kissed him hard on the cheek. He was wearing enough deodorant for a platoon.

"I will be back, George, when I have worked through all of this. I won't be a bitch forever," I promised.

"You're my lady," he replied. There were tears rimming his eyes.

He walked off up Beacon Hill toward the State House in the direction of the Putnam.

I activated the side door and lift and was rolling off of the grid when Barney ran out the front door. There was building litter on both sides of the brick walkway.

"The new elevator," Barney explained.

Lucille hustled out to get my belongings, trying not to sniffle, and my mother stood in the entrance crying uncontrollably.

"Toni, I'm so sorry," she stammered, "I promised and promised myself I wouldn't do this." She kissed me and hugged me. I felt terrible for her. It had been like this every day at the hospital. It was not at all my beautiful mother with her lovely transparent complexion, her proudly tilted head, and the self-confidence of a genuine aristocrat. I felt a terrible pang of guilt. We crowded into a tiny new three-story elevator whose construction absolutely ruined the entryway and everything else old and lovely in the stately town house.

* * *

There was a ceramic ledge in the third floor bathroom which prevented the wheelchair from rolling into my favorite shower. I had undressed in my bedroom, and wheeled naked into the bathroom. When I saw the ledge I grabbed a towel bar to swing out onto the floor, it gave away and I crashed down among broken tiles and plaster. I threw the bar at the wall breaking more tiles, then used my arms to crawl into the shower, reached up and blasted myself with the water.

I sat sprawled on the shower floor, biting on a washcloth. Finally I soaped up and scrubbed. A pain somewhere around my heart seized me when I noticed my legs were withering from disuse. It didn't help that the plastic urine bag had torn away on the ledge and a yellow puddle of urine was spilling over the white pile carpet. The brown neoprene urine catheter still disappeared between my legs like some horrible worm. I took several deep breaths and the pain eased. I sat watching the water run down the drain.

Barney pounded on the door and started to come in. "No!" I shouted at him. "Not you! Get mother up here. I don't want you to see me like this!" I saw a stricken look on Barney's face as he closed the door.

I was pulling myself back over the ledge when Jeanette hurried in. "Oh Toni," she gasped, putting both hands to her face.

"Mother, I'm fine, don't be so upset," I snapped.

I pulled the wheelchair toward me and turned my back to it. "Just steady the chair as I lift myself up," I instructed, reaching back for the armrests. When I felt the chair steady I lifted myself quickly and plopped into the seat. It was surprisingly easy after all of George's instructions…we had been through the routine daily in physical therapy. I now had more upper body strength than before the accident, which even then had been twice that of most women. Give credit to Barney's ancestors, again, I thought.

"Mother, please get my terry robe from my bedroom and bring the kit they sent from the hospital…we have to do some water-works repair."

Jeanette hovered around me as I dressed for supper, insisted on combing my hair, her hands trembling as she did so. Finally she started crying.

"Oh, Toni, what have I done?" she sobbed. She sat down on the bed beside the wheelchair and put her face in her hands, the brush clattered to the floor.

"If you're thinking about that argument we had, Mother, I want you to forget it. We were both angry. It meant nothing."

"It means nothing when you accuse your daughter of having the mannerisms of a French prostitute? Oh, Toni how could I? I'm responsible for...this! I am!"

I pulled her toward me and she leaned against my chest, sobbing like a child. The wheelchair slid back a foot, I wondered if we were both going to end up on the floor.

"Nonsense, Mother," I said. I sat her back on the bed before we went wheeling across the room. She looked at me, her tear-streaked face twisted in pain.

"I was jealous, Toni. Of you and your father. He's so proud of you! And you can do no wrong in his eyes. I had a jealous fit...and now...this!"

I took her hands in mine, she clutched me, her fingers twisting and turning like agonized snakes. "Mother, I'm not all Barney," I said gently. "Sure, I'm tall, and strong, and love to win, but that's not all of me; I'm you too, you know. I just hope I have half of your decency and charm. And spirit. All those ancestors, Mother. Lavoisier? Discovered and named oxygen? Right? Your ancestor. Am I right? Walked to the guillotine with his head held high...isn't that what you've always told me? Where do you think I get my brains, Mother? Barney says his ancestors were mining coal before they walked upright."

Jeanette had to laugh at the old family joke. She dabbed her eyes.

"Come, on Jeanette," I said, "Let's get ourselves fixed up and go down and have supper with the old boy." She smiled and hugged me hard. My mother is a wonderful woman.

*   *   *

I waited until supper was over before I dropped the bomb. "Barney," I said, trying to control a tremor that kept creeping into my voice, "I'm going out to Ohio to see if they can help me."

"Toni, I know all about this wild idea. That boy...the medical student..."

"Vincent Antonelli."

"Yes Antonelli. He came to see me...I grant him that much. And I listened. I listened very carefully, Toni. You know that I can do that, and I don't allow my emotions to cloud rational decisions."

I knew what was happening. "You're going to tell me that you forbid me to do this," I said. "You've had your mind made up before I ever walked...wheeled in here." That started Jeanette sniffling again.

"Toni, I talked to all the specialists. Aaron Scheckler is an irresponsible drunk. He's a dangerous man."

"So you sent him off to the osteopaths? Did you tell *them* that?"

I could see his temper rising. Barnard Putnam on the attack is not pleasant to watch.

"You've failed to meet this disaster adequately, Toni. You know you have. I don't intend to be cruel, but the sooner you accept all of this and find a new life, the better. The people who understand these things and deal with them professionally feel they've failed with you also."

"Vincent Antonelli has talked to...."

"Yes! Hasn't he though. Do you know what others think of this meddling young man, Toni? They're convinced he's as responsible as anyone for your being stuck in denial. He's no different from the 'friend' who's always offering an alcoholic a 'friendly' drink. He's worse than a parasite. I sent him away after giving him a piece of my mind. If I hear of him being around you I will have him arrested!"

"Barney, does it occur to you that I'm twenty years old? That I'm an adult who can make my own decisions?" I asked.

"Not in this matter, Toni. It's too important." Barney poured from the silver coffeepot in front of him. His hand was shaking and he spilled most of it. I could see he was furious.

"Damn!" he snapped.

"Barney, I'm going." I said. "It's a procedure that has little risk, and several of the Putnam neurologists think it has promise. I'm going."

"That's not what the neurologists tell me," Barney snapped.

"That's because you're Barnard Putnam III, who will ruin their careers in a nanosecond if anything goes wrong. Who would dare tell you this was a good idea?"

"We'll discuss this more in the morning, Toni. I'll sleep on it."

"That will be too late, Barney, I'm leaving for Ohio tonight. There's no time to be lost."

"What? How...."

"In the van. I'll drive out so I will have transportation out there."

"I suppose this Antonelli is going with you?"

"No."

"You're going *alone*?"

"Oh, my God, Toni," said my mother. "Alone. In *your* condition? Are you out of your mind?"

"I agree," said Barney. "Quite simply, Toni, I forbid this madness. You're not yourself."

"Are you telling me you're going to lock me up?" I said. I couldn't believe this.

"If I have to. Yes. I would do that."

The dark shadows below Barney's heavy black brows accented the deep sad creases in his cheeks. His chin quivered. I'd never seen that. What was I doing to my mother and father? Was I actually crazy? I wasn't far from it, I knew that much. But I compressed my lips and clenched my teeth. I was not going to be talked out of this. There was silence for several minutes before my father pushed back shakily from the table. "I...I'm going up to bed," he said, rubbing his forehead. "I have a terrible headache." Jeanette darted out of her chair and went around to him.

"Toni," she said, "I'm going upstairs with your father. He hasn't had a decent night of sleep since all this happened. On the telephone day and night, beside himself with worry and grief. He's not himself. I'll be back down in several minutes."

I sat glumly at the table, watching the lights on Louisburg Square. I heard Jeanette rustling behind me as she returned. "Toni, are you packed?" she asked quietly. I heard a chair slide out as she sat down.

"Before I came down," I replied.

"Do you have to go tonight?"

"If I don't go right now, I never will."

"Then I'll go with you."

"No, Mother, that wouldn't work and you know it. I think I'm losing my mind. It's hopeless. Barney will have the State Police bring me back before I get to Natick."

"I'll take care of Barney," she said quietly.

I pulled out of Louisburg Square, angled across Dartmouth Street and caught I-90 beyond Copley Place. I headed west. Darkness was ahead of me as the spring twilight faded from the cloudless sky.

HOSTAGE!

I will say this for the converted Dodge Caravan; it worked. I had my special gel-foam whoopee pad in the wheelchair, the steering wheel had a knob on it that allowed sharp turns with one hand, the accelerator/brake arm was smooth as silk. A panel separated the driver's area from a narrow bed behind, made up and turned back by Lucille, "in case," Barney had explained, "you might get stuck somewhere without handicap facilities."

That really made me wonder if Barney had known all along that I would be taking off from Louisburg Square until I could get things sorted out. Barney is very keen at reading minds. He has made a pile of money doing just that. The other thing he does is play it very close to the vest. I wasn't very far past Sturbridge before I missed Barney something awful.

The sliding side entryway took up much of the space on the passenger side of the van, there was a chemical toilet behind that contraption, and across from the driver's center console was a huge adjustable reclining chair. Barney had seen to it that nothing was left out. There was a cellular telephone plugged into one of the accessory outlets, a tiny percolator in the other, a compass in the unit over my head, and a compact disk player in front of me. I was on the Wilbur Cross Highway when Jeanette called.

"Toni, your father is sound asleep. He's fine, just exhausted," she said.

Jeanette sounded much better. "When are you going to get some sleep?" she demanded. Now I *knew* she was feeling better.

"Mother, I just got started," I replied.

"Toni, it's almost midnight. You stop driving and get some sleep. I'm going to do the same."

"I'll call tomorrow, mother," I replied.

"That boy...Antonelli? He called. He's worried. He's trying to arrange to get out...wherever it is you're going. I'll call the Dean myself in the morning if there is any difficulty in his being excused from classes. Isn't he about finished with school, anyway?"

"Just several days, mother," I replied.

"I think it is a good idea that he gets out there with you...even if Barney doesn't like him," she said firmly.

My mother believes I need a man around. Women from her background usually have several.

* * *

By four o'clock in the morning I'd made it to the Pennsylvania Turnpike at Carlisle. I was exhausted and disoriented by the heavy truck traffic from New Jersey and beyond. The motel was speckled with street grime, the lobby lit by a single bulb on the registration desk. I had a noisy struggle getting through the plate glass entrance door. The noise brought out a thick-bodied man wearing an old fashioned undershirt and pajama pants. He needed a shave and his eyes were heavy with sleep. "Jeezus!" he yelled at me, "take it *easy*, lady."

"You have showers that take a wheelchair?" I snapped. "Because you sure don't give a shit if anybody can get into this place."

"I got the showers. What I don't have is the forty thousand bucks it cost me to put in all that crap," he replied. I could see we were never going to be very close.

But there wasn't any choice. What I needed was a shower, an enema, a new urine bag, and four hour's sleep.

The next day was sunny and warm and I felt a lot better. Dogwoods were blooming all over the mountains. I was getting used to the violent wind gusts from passing trucks.

By noon I was ready to leave the turnpike for I-70 at New Stanton. The attendant at the toll booth looked me over carefully. "Mind if we have a look in the van?" he asked casually. When I shrugged, he took my money and the toll ticket, gave me the change and motioned me through. I pulled over to the edge of the blacktop where two state troopers leaned on the fender of a cruiser with its lights flickering across the top. One of them walked over to the van.

"What's going on?" I asked.

"Would you open the back, please?" he asked. I flipped the switch and the door slid sideways. He looked underneath the van, then placed his hands on the grid and vaulted inside. He felt the surface of the bed, walked to the back and kicked a large canvas duffel I had thrown against the back wall. He came forward, hitching up his gun belt like he was getting ready for a gunfight at the OK corral.

"If you're looking for drugs, there aren't any," I snapped.

"Lady, if I was looking for drugs there would be a dog sniffing this van and I'd already be filling out the paperwork." As he came past the partition he glanced under the wheelchair. What was he looking for, a midget? "May I see your handicap license and the insurance, please?" He looked them over, glancing up at me twice, then hopped out the side door. "Don't pick up any hitchhikers," he said, and motioned me away.

There was a rest stop a mile down I-70. I'd been sniffing myself for the last hour and didn't like what I smelled. I think I was having a problem with what was called at the Putnam, "involuntary evacuation". My colon still was not completely housebroken. The more I smelled, the less I liked it. I pulled up to the curb, opened the door, started the lift, rolled furiously to the back, grabbed the gym bag with all the paraphernalia, rolled off of the lift as it hit the ground and pumped myself over into the rest room.

It took half an hour to clean up the mess. There was dark yellow baby shit all over everything. After I got myself cleaned up and washed off, ignoring one nosy tourist after another, I pulled on old blue polyester running pants and a crimson Harvard pullover, fighting the twisting of the chair as I threshed around.

I scrubbed off the soiled clothes, wrung them out as best I could and stuffed them in the gym bag. I was furious. I pumped the handrails so hard on the way back to the van that one leg kept flopping off the footrest. When I yanked it back the chair spun out of control, threatening to crash into the bushes. I stormed back up the ramp and into the van, threw the bag toward the back, wheeled into position, fired up the motor and shot out onto the highway. I was two miles down the road, and putting the van into cruise when I realized I *was not alone.*

It was a just a very faint scrape on the divider between the driver's seat and the cot behind. Then I smelled sweat. Heavy unwashed male sweat. The hair at the nape of my neck rose and my heart started to pound. I looked in the side-view mirror. It was no help. I started to look behind the screen, but swerved wildly on the road and wrestled with the wheel. I moved the hand control to release the cruise and started to brake as I headed for the berm.

"Don't do that," grunted a coarse voice behind my ear. "Keep going or you're a dead woman."

I steered back onto the roadway, still slowing down. "Keep it at sixty-five," the voice insisted. I picked up speed.

"That's better. I think if you're smart enough you might still die of old age."

He slid from behind the screen and into the passenger seat. He placed a 12 gauge pump shotgun on the carpet beside his seat. When he saw me staring at it he said quietly, "This morning that belonged to a farmer. Used to be a farmer. His brains is all over his barn." He smiled wickedly.

He was a small man, less than 140 pounds, dressed in a blue denim work shirt that was far too large for him, and jeans rolled up on skinny white legs and gathered in heavy folds with a belt at his waist. "Yeah," he said, watching me with an evil grin. "His clothes, too."

He took his time adjusting the seat to suit himself while I struggled to get control of myself.

"I got two weapons," he continued, "that," he jerked his head toward the shotgun, "and this." He extended a skinny arm, showing me the palm of his hand. There was a small knife lying in it. In the center of the highly polished ebony handle was a bright silver button. He pressed the button with a dirty thumbnail and a shining steel blade swished out with a soft click. The blade glittered in the sunlight.

"Do anything stupid, lady, and I'm going to cut so many strips down the sides of your face you'll think you're the American flag." He smiled again. "I'm running," he said simply. "I ain't never going back. You help me, you live. You get me caught, you die first."

He opened the glove compartment and felt around. "Some of you cripples carry a gun around," he said. "That would really be stupid." He sat back with a satisfied look on his face. He smelled like something dead. As he moved or raised an arm a new wave would come across, so pungent it strangled me.

Thoughts raced around in my mind like cornered rats. What I wouldn't give to see that state trooper coming down the aisle with a hand on his holster. The last time I saw him he was leaning on the fender of his cruiser, joking with his partner as I pulled away.

What could I possibly do? If I signaled a trucker, I would be a bloody mess by the time someone got to me. Even if someone had sense enough to call the Highway Patrol and they set up a roadblock, it would be the same. If I wrecked the van, he would run, I would be left. The obvious choice I wasn't ready for. I wasn't going to kill myself over him. Not yet anyway.

We went through a tunnel. I could see him grinning at me in the semi-darkness. The stench was overpowering. He must have known what I was thinking.

"I run a long way last night," he said. He settled down and seemed to doze, but startled awake each time a heavy truck passed. He had a narrow pinched face and deep eye sockets as if the flesh underneath was eaten away. The more I thought about it, the more certain I was he was going to kill me. That was his best chance. He wouldn't take the van. Too obvious and too quirky. We'd drive until he started to panic about whatever was spinning around in his mind, then he would take me where I wouldn't be found and do it. They would still be looking everywhere for him, he would use the time to find another farmer and better transportation. Time was his problem.

I had two problems. I needed a weapon, and I needed opportunity.

*   *   *

We rode for over an hour in doomed silence. He had already sensed I was not going to melt or panic. I could see that begin to frighten him. "You still do sex?" he asked slyly. "You know, you must be good at *something*." It was a threat. It was meant to terrify.

"With who?" I asked.

"With *me*, you dumb bitch," he snarled.

"You'd have to take a bath first," I replied.

He looked at me with renewed interest. "Why hell," he said, trying to sound coy, "that ain't no problem, really. I'll ponder that."

His hand darted over, sliding it quickly under my pullover, rubbing around on my breast. I didn't flinch, just looked at him.

"Yeah," he said, withdrawing his hand. Maybe I can find a little lake or something.

Take a little swim."

We crossed the long bridge at Wheeling. "What's your name?" I asked him, trying to sound interested.

"You don't need to know any name for what you're gonna do, lady," he replied with that evil all-knowing grin. He was watching the roadside like a ferret, interested in every small pond or creek. He pointed at a sign for a state park.

"In there," he commanded. "Most of them places has a pond or something."

The park was deserted. A sign said "No overnight camping". In the background was a small pond choked with reeds.

TERROR AT THE LAKE

"Back there," he said. "Where that road runs out of sight." I pulled along the road beside the pond. "Now get out of this thing."

I opened the sliding door as he snatched the shotgun and jumped out of the passenger side. He watched me descend on the grid. "Close it up," he said. The grid rose back inside the van and the door slid shut.

He had stripped off his clothes. His skin was dead white all over. Without taking his eyes from me he backed into the edge of the pond, sat down and splashed in the water. I pulled off my top. "Hey, look at you!" he shouted, leaping up and sending a shower of spray through the heavy cattails. He charged at me from the edge of the water.

"Man, look at them tits!" He bent down over the wheelchair, breathing heavily, grabbing a handful of hair behind my head, pulling me toward him.

"What the f…!" he yelped, then his voice was muffled. I had yanked him forward and snapped my pullover over his head. He stumbled, lost his footing, and I flipped him around and wrapped my arms around the cloth, pinning his arms to his sides. He twisted savagely, trying to break the hold, I locked my hands together around the front of his chest and squeezed with every bit of strength I had. Fear and fury rose, bursting in my head and shooting throughout my body, blazing in an intensity as real as a bolt of lightening. He was *not* big, my brain said, he was *not* a skier, my senses screamed, he smelled like filth *and he was not as strong as I was!!*

In that instant both of us knew. He swore and screamed. I yanked tighter with all of my strength. He threshed sideways and I used the momentum to smash his chest against the arm of the wheelchair. I felt his chest give way with a sickening crunch and he yelped. He gasped for a breath so I yanked and smashed again, feeling more crunching. Then we spun sideways crazily, rolling out of the wheelchair onto the ground. After a stunned moment I realized I still had him! I squeezed with everything I had. I knew my life depended on it.

He whimpered and stopped struggling. When I relaxed slightly to take a breath he twisted and kicked and was almost free! I bore down again, silently and grimly, determined to think of nothing else except how hard I could squeeze. I began to feel weak and dizzy.

He startled me with a violent fit of coughing followed by loud bubbling sounds coming out of the cloth twisted over his head. Then he retched and vomited.

I held tight and waited. He went limp…I was certain it was another trick. I waited longer. My hands were numb where they gripped around his chest. There were more weak coughs. I squeezed tighter. White hot fury lashed and flickered over and around me. I gritted my teeth and squeezed harder. I felt like I was consumed by fire. So this is what hell is like?

I waited what seemed forever and then cautiously released one hand and worked the pullover off of his head and looked at his face. Blood was running from his nose, bloody foam from his mouth, and his eyes were rolled back with only whites showing. I shuddered and threw him off only to find I was so weak all I could do was lay in the muddy grass and watch him. If he looked at me or moved, I was going to choke him, and keep on choking him if it was the last thing I ever did on this earth.

He did nothing but groan and cough up bright pink foam. I rolled away from him and pulled myself up into the wheelchair. I snatched away the filthy cloth top, crumpled it up on my lap, fumbled for the remote and sat trembling uncontrollably for an eternity while the side door slowly opened and the lift whirred down. My grip on the wheel rails kept sliding off and I swayed crazily as the grid lifted me up and into the van. I pulled a soft pack out from under the bed and got out a clean sweatshirt and put it on. Then I struggled up front, locked all the doors, started the engine and backed out throwing gravel.

I hit the entrance to the Interstate, flipping down the visor, looking at myself as I jammed down the accelerator arm and gunned down the highway. My face was stained with tears and mud. Over the top was a tangle of black hair and leaves. I had just killed a man and I certainly looked the part. I forced myself to quiet down and breathe deeply. I clenched the wheel trying to control the trembling. In the rear mirror I watched the dark aisle of the van, certain I would see that skinny stinking little monster lunging toward me.

THE STATE PATROLMAN

I tried to drive but the real world kept fading in and out; I found myself far over on the berm careening toward the guard rail. I twisted frantically on the steering knob, fish-tailed back onto the blacktop, a huge truck swerved away from me with a monstrous horn blast, tires screamed and metal squealed as the truck rocked back and forth as it shot past. The horn continued long after the back end of the truck had passed.

I drove on the gravel berm, my hands so weak I could barely control the van. Exiting on a lonely ramp leading to a gravel crossroad, I stopped and leaned over the wheel, my body and arms shaking and twitching. I could not tear my eyes away from the rear view mirrors, dreading what I *knew* I was going to see. I was certain he was sneaking up the aisle of the van or running down the road after me.

I turned on the heater to stop the shivering. It didn't help even after the van felt like an oven and sweat was streaming down my face. If I wasn't a murderer, if he was *alive,* he would find me and *cut me to ribbons*! I could feel the knife slicing down my face on one side, then he gripped my chin and slowly twisted so he could cut the other side. I started screaming and that helped. I screamed until I was exhausted. I turned off the heater, opened the window, leaned back and watched the busy freeway below. I watched it until late afternoon while I made myself remember every race I had won, and close ones I had lost. The smallest details. I found finally I could take a deep breath and started to feel human. Then I got the hiccups and held my breath to make them go away. Like Barney taught me to do when I cried and got the hiccups when I was little. I put the van in gear and crossed the lonely farm road and headed back onto I-70. I was finally able to think.

*   *   *

After I don't know how many miles, I narrowed it down to two choices. If I got on the cell phone to state cops I would never see Athens, Ohio. I would be detained. I would be questioned. There would be proceedings. At least four Boston lawyers and Barney, after which I would be back in Louisburg Square in my wheelchair…forever. Or I could clean myself up and keep going.

After that there was never any doubt in my mind. At the next rest stop I made it into the women's rest room, stripped for the third time that day, soaked up a large mat of paper towels and washed all over with cold water. I combed my hair. I kept watching nervously for some tourist to come in, but it was late afternoon and there were no visitors.

I cleaned my fingernails and brushed my teeth, then fished around in the duffel and struggled into a fresh pair of jeans, a tee shirt and a black turtleneck. The muddy pullover was sticky with nauseating bloody saliva. I considered dumping it but decided that wouldn't be smart. Already I was thinking like an ax murderess. I stuffed it in the duffel. Then I hit the road for Athens.

I was feeling pretty good about all of this, was planning a stop in Zanesville to see if eating something might help, was actually heading into the exit when I saw a patrol car in the outer lane suddenly slow down and swerve over behind me. He followed me onto the ramp.

Before we reached the crossroad he turned on his cherry light. My heart sank.

The officer sat in his cruiser for several minutes, then stepped out, walking very tall and straight up along the van. I rolled down my window. He wore a smoky-bear hat, had iron gray hair, and large black sunglasses shielding a heavily tanned face. "Afternoon," he said pleasantly. "May I see your license?"

My hand shook as I handed it out the window. He studied it.

"Where are you headed, Miss Putnam?"

"Athens. I…am supposed to get some special treatment there."

The cop nodded as if all of this was very agreeable. "A park ranger found a naked man in a campground back about seventy miles," he said in the same conversational tone, "you know anything about that?"

"Why should I?"

"The little fellow claims he knows you."

I felt an enormous surge of relief knowing that skinny stinking cockroach was alive. I could feel the color coming back into my face and the nausea subsiding. I realized I wasn't an ax murderess after all. It felt really good…like I'd just beat Heidi Fleisch in a downhill.

"Well, he doesn't," I replied, in what I hoped was a convincing tone. Had I lied yet? I didn't think so.

"He killed a farmer over in Pennsylvania last night," replied the cop. I did my best to look surprised.

"Was in prison for killing his wife," he continued, "and almost killed the driver of the laundry truck he hid in to escape. Cut the man's face and then stabbed him twice, apparently just for the hell of it." He paused, waiting for a response, hitching his belt and then leaning back on the edge of the window. I did my best to keep my eyes steady on those black glasses and look innocent.

"What the Pennsylvania Patrol wants to know is how he got over here."

The patrolman handed back the license. "As a matter of fact, they would like to know how he got naked, and how he got half his ribs on one side busted and a lung full of blood."

"A wild animal?" I asked the officer. I kept looking straight into those opaque sunglasses. I was feeling a lot better. What were they going to charge me with? Breaking ribs?

For the first time he smiled. I'll bet he has a good looking wife.

"Oh, there's no doubt about that, Miss Putnam," he replied. "No damn doubt about that at all. What they want to know is what sort of wild animal." The smile didn't waver.

"Why do you think I know anything about any of this?"

"Why, Miss Putnam, while the little creep was waiting for the Life Flight helicopter he gave a pretty good description…that is when he could get any breath. Also the truckers been watching the roads in four states for us, and one of them said he thought he saw a handicapped van like this one pull out of that park going like a bat out of hell. I'm following up on that…"

"Must've been another van." I thought I sounded pretty convincing.

He removed the sunglasses, polished them with a red bandana handkerchief, put them back on and settled them carefully. He placed both hands on the edge of the window. "You're the kid who won the bronze medal in the Olympics three years ago, aren't you."

"Yes sir."

"My daughter has a poster on her wall of your winning run."

"That was a very long time ago."

"I read about the accident. Sorry."

"How did you read about that?"

"Sheely, you know, ran a story in the Boston paper. The AP picked it up. We got it in Cambridge."

First I need Coach Pearce with all his push-ups, I thought, now Sheely. It could be those guys are worth something after all. The cop noticed I was uncomfortable.

"Are you all right , Miss Putnam?"

"Never been better."

"Well, I've been on the Cambridge station twenty years, Miss Putnam, and, believe me, you're the prettiest liar of them all. And we get lied to a lot. You go on your way. If the judge or someone wants to talk to you, I think I can find you, right?" He glanced at the darkening sky, stripped off the sun glasses again and slipped them into the pocket below his badge. His eyes were dark brown, just like Antonelli's. There were deep creases at the corners.

"Wild animal," he said to himself, the crinkles deepening. "Now I can retire. I've heard it all."

He walked back to his cruiser whistling. He waved as he went past.

I pulled into Athens at ten thirty. I'd come down through the hills watching the evening fog spill and swirl through the valleys in the twilight. I was stuffed with a good Ohio beefsteak and the Budget Host Coach Inn on U.S. 50 had great handicap facilities. My luck was bound to change.

"WE ARE NOT PRIDEFUL"

William Henderson, the Dean of the Ohio College of Osteopathic Medicine, was a small man with a very round head covered with wispy gray hair. He wore a look of perpetual frustration. He diddled with a paper clip while he tried to decide what to say. His first complaint was about Scheckler, which did not surprise me.

"He was arrested, you know, Miss Putnam, before he ever got here," Henderson said in an offended tone. "He was driving that decrepit Econoline without a driver's license, no tail-lights, and that ape in the back." Henderson rubbed his thinning hair. "I had to go over to Cambridge to get him out of jail. Thank God he hadn't been drinking. That problem, by the way has been under good control here. Not perfect, but much better."

I realized Henderson was trying to tell me he thought he got a better deal than Barney thought he was getting. "I'm very sorry, Dr. Henderson," I said, hoping I sounded as if I meant it.

"Miss Putnam, I know exactly what Barney thought he was doing," he continued slyly, "but I took Dr. Scheckler with my eyes wide open. I checked him out very thoroughly…with a great many of his fellow professionals. We…the faculty and I…wanted to give him another chance." He tossed the paperclip aside. "And we have not been disappointed. His lectures have been gems…he has given several and the students love him…he has quite a wry sense of humor."

"Your father and I were undergraduates together," Henderson explained. "Barney went off to business school, and I went to medical school."

Why do older men always want to tell you things you already know, I wondered, trying to concentrate. "I hear you were great friends," I said. That always worked.

Henderson sat up and seemed to take heart. "Barney's been calling. I want you to be very careful, Miss Putnam. You must check with me about everything. We are trying to give Dr. Scheckler the chance he wants so desperately. All of the safeguards and restrictions are in place, we have been very careful about that. If it doesn't work out now, we want him to continue with more…basic research and to be here with us as a fine teacher. We don't want him to be hurt, we don't want anyone of his…subjects…to be hurt, and I don't want this institution to be hurt. Do you understand me? There is a great deal at stake."

"I'm very anxious to see Dr. Scheckler…to get started, Dr. Henderson."

"Of course. We've arranged for you to stay here on West Green?"

"Yes, Dr. Henderson, in Wilson Hall, if I have it right," I replied.

"You'll room in the dormitory with Amy Yoder," Henderson said, "she's the other patient of Dr. Scheckler's. Actually it's very reassuring to me to have you here." He looked at me shrewdly. "You know, to be with Amy. You can be a great help to her, I'm sure."

"What do you mean by that, Dr. Henderson?"

The Dean shifted uncomfortably in his chair and started to fiddle again with the paper clip, avoiding my eyes. If he had been doing a business deal with Barney that would have been a signal to attack. "Amy is…different, Miss Putnam; very innocent." He looked up to see if I understood. I didn't.

"You mean she's simple-minded or something?" I asked.

"Oh my no! Far from it. It's just that she knows nothing about the outside world. She's in some ways very like a wild-child. You know of such cases, I'm sure?" he replied.

"Anyone who's taken freshman psychology knows about wild children, Dr. Henderson. Tarzan included."

Henderson smiled. His thin lips barely parted. "Perhaps I put that too strongly. Amy belongs to a very…fundamental group, there are many different such groups in Pennsylvania and Ohio, as you know…Quakers, Mennonites, Amish, Shakers…all sorts of flavors from worldly and sophisticated, to some who do not use electricity or machinery at all. Amy belongs to a small group over in Vinton County who stay very much to themselves, live from subsistence farming and wood cutting. Wonderful people, really, but Amy has not the least idea what's going on here, I mean what Dr. Scheckler intends to do and so forth. It's all absolutely based on faith. That makes me very uncomfortable. The fact you're here will change all that, I hope." Henderson took a deep breath, as if he had been relieved of a very heavy load.

"That's it? This Amy is the only…patient here waiting for…whatever it is he's going to do?" I didn't like the sound of this. "I mean, no others?"

Henderson pursed his lips. "That's all he has permission to study," he said with emphasis. The National Institute of Health is very specific. He…has had one failure."

"So I hear."

"Be very careful, Miss Putnam," he warned. "I want you to be very careful about all of this. I want to know about any therapy before it happens. I may want another neurologist to concur."

"Yes sir," I replied.

"Did you have a pleasant drive down from Boston?"

"Delightful."

"This is a nice season to see the campus. I hope you'll be happy here."

"Thank you, Dr. Henderson."

I decided to leave my van in the visitor's lot and turned toward the small quadrangle of bright green grass in front of the building, trying to pick the blacktop pathway that would lead to the right residence hall. The intersections were confusing at first view, running many directions among fresh plots on newly planted summer flowers. I found Wilson on my third attempt.

The dorm room had Amy Yoder's name on the door, the door was ajar, a passing student told me Amy was in the shower down the hall. As I shoved into the steamy room one wheel skidded on the wet tiles and I slammed sideways into the swinging door. Amy sat naked in her dripping wheelchair, bending forward as she dried her legs and feet with a large white towel. She ignored my swearing.

She was softly rounded everywhere, skin very white, breasts large, plump without being fat. When she straightened, her face was deeply tanned with a sharp line where the white started again at her forehead. Her hair was soft brown, hanging in tangles over her shoulders. As she vigorously dried her hair her small hands were as brown as her cheeks. The plastic bag half filled with pale yellow urine was tucked between her legs and attached to a tan neoprene catheter which disappeared into damp brown hair…the badge of our exclusive sorority. She smiled in recognition.

"You have to be Antoinette Putnam," she said, her eyes sparkling. Then she said shyly, "I've never met a famous person before."

Amy Yoder was very beautiful in a very different way. Her expression and manner seemed of another time or place. Not here. Not naked in a wheelchair in a college dormitory.

Piled neatly on a bench lay a one-piece cotton shift, a dark brown dress with hook-and-eye fasteners, and a pair of brown slippers. Beyond the pile perched a black bonnet edged with dark brown ribbon which explained the sharp tan line on her forehead. Her manner conveyed not the slightest hint of concern or self-consciousness. Her light green eyes were untroubled, her movements slow and without hesitation. She very deliberately dried herself, almost as if she was sending some sort of silent message. Finally she pulled the cotton shift over her head, then the dress; followed by all the grotesque lifting and turning to get them down over her body and legs. Movements I knew so well and hated. I knew better than offer help, just as she had known to take no notice of my clumsy entrance. Henderson was right. She radiated simplicity and peace.

"Amy, I'm not famous," I argued, "I'm just a woman athlete who was very lucky."

"Well, anyway," replied Amy, "I know we're going to be great friends." She paused. "Did you bring in your things? If not, all of the students want to help. They're very excited to have somebody here who has won a medal and goes to Harvard and all; I've heard them talking about you. You'll have to tell me all about Harvard. I'm afraid I don't know anything about it at all." She hesitated. "We don't believe in schooling beyond the eighth grade, you know." Her smile told me she was not apologizing, only explaining.

I looked at her carefully to see if she was ribbing me. Apparently she wasn't. What would Barney think about that , I wondered. Somebody who didn't know *anything* about Harvard? "I'll bring the stuff in later," I said. "There isn't much. I don't care about moving in. I want to see Dr. Scheckler as soon as possible."

"We'll go over together. I get my last tests today. I'm almost ready for Priscilla and her virus."

"Doctor Henderson was concerned that you don't understand all you should about Priscilla and the virus," I replied.

"Oh, no, I don't know anything about that at all," Amy said. "What I know is that Dr. Scheckler arrived here almost the very day I needed him. We believe...my people believe...it's a sign. I don't have to know anything more than that." She was very serious in her quiet way. "It would be prideful for me to think I could understand what Dr. Scheckler is doing for me," she continued, as if she was lecturing a child. "Or for me to question him. He's going to cure me. He can do what he wills."

"Oh, Amy, that's not…"

She held up her hand to silence me. "We're not prideful, Miss Putnam," she said firmly. "We don't pretend to know what we cannot know, we're not embarrassed by nakedness, we dress plain because we're not beautiful, we do not brag, we do not covet. We are Children of God."

She finished dressing and we wheeled down the hallway together, students pressing against the walls and smiling and nodding as we passed. She seemed to sail along carefree, her black bonnet framing her placid expression.

I had a surge of unreality. I was trapped in a nightmare taking place a hundred years ago! This was some nuthouse where I had been committed! A skinny white monster was creeping toward the corner of the hallway, a knife glistening in his clawed hand.

THE MESSENGER VIRUS

Same old Aaron Scheckler. Wrinkled slacks, frayed tweed jacket and expression of suppressed anger. The laboratory was bare bones...cement block walls, Formica benches, stainless steel centrifuges, a binocular microscope, esoteric glassware, and Priscilla threshing around in a glass-walled room in the back. There was even a dry ice sump giving off wispy vapors. A Frankenstein movie.

Scheckler was interested in Amy, barely giving me a nod of recognition, I wondered if it was payback for the way he had been treated in Barney's office. He had Amy strip to the waist, spent a long time listening to her heart and lungs, peered into her eyes after turning off the lights, moved with quick self-important steps to snap the lights back on and then a slow methodical neurological examination. I knew all about that.

The expression on his face at the pause following every small pinprick gave him a comical air, like a magician in a sideshow. Perhaps pull out a rabbit from somewhere, or a half dollar from behind Amy's ear. He enlisted me to apply a tuning fork to her kneecaps while he tapped with a rubber mallet on the tendons at her elbows and ankles and scraped his fingernail along the sole of her foot, causing the toes to curl and the leg to jerk away. Amy watched contentedly from her wheelchair. He darted between Amy and his desk, making copious notes.

Then he then did the same to me, making more notes and nodding to himself as he worked. He even had Amy use the tuning fork on me, which seemed to amuse him.

He drew several vials of blood from Amy, inspected them in the light, shook them, seemed satisfied, and dropped them into the centrifuge. "All right," he said, "both of you put your things on. Amy, we're finished, you go along. I want to talk with Miss Putnam."

"When....? Dr. Scheckler," asked Amy.

"I have some cell studies to do on this blood, Amy. If those and the routine tests are what I expect, we'll give you your last tablets tomorrow, and Priscilla will get her injection Monday."

"And then?" Amy asked.

"We would be ready for you about four hours later."

"That will be a real blessing," said Amy, and she wheeled herself out of the front door.

Scheckler poured a cup of coffee from a large beaker resting beneath a filter device. He motioned to me, waving his hand in the air.

"Do you know anything about that girl?" he asked. He slid a drawer open, selected several vials and what looked like a very large hypodermic needle, dropped into a chair beside me and wrapped a rubber tourniquet around my arm.

"We haven't had much chance to talk," I replied.

Scheckler swiped an alcohol sponge at the inside of my elbow and slid in the needle. Blood poured into the vial attached to it. He leaned across me, picked up his coffee cup and sipped on it as he watched the vial fill. Then he slipped on another vial and the blood poured in again.

"She's the most innocent person I've ever known, Toni. Belongs to a very conservative branch of some sort of church. Trusts me absolutely. It weighs very heavily on me."

"You won't have that problem with me," I replied.

Scheckler laughed. More of a cackle than anything else. "Thank God," he replied. "What do you want to know about all of this?" He attached a *third* vial.

"Every bit I can understand."

"Well, I assume you know that genes can be transcribed and made to operate even after they've been transferred from one species to another?"

"Yes."

"And that I've modified an enterovirus, actually a polio virus mutant. It retains its ability to enter by way of the gut, but has also characteristics of the rhinoviruses, being shed in the nasal discharges when invited to do so by reduced resistance." Scheckler paused and studied my expression. "Are you following me?" Scheckler walked over and placed the vials in the centrifuge and turned it on.

"You just lost me."

"Toni, you know how cold sores appear…when the patient has a cold?" He chuckled at his own joke. "That herpes virus is loafing up in the brain until resistance drops with the cold infection whereupon the virus races down the nerves from the brain and makes a large sore on the lips or tongue. It's a parasite, you see. It lives in nervous tissue. The cold sore is how it spreads itself to other hosts. Some women even have them with their menstrual periods."

"So?"

"So the virus I have modified does much the same thing. Four hours after a dose of an immuno-suppressant, Priscilla gets a 'cold' and sheds a lot of virus. The virus we want to give to you."

"Why?"

Scheckler was irritated. "To carry the myelin repair gene I've placed in the viral nucleus so it can get into your spine and repair your injury."

"You mean the virus carries the gene inside of me?" Carries the myelin repair gene from the intestine to my spinal cord?"

"Yes. Very quickly, I might add."

"And, we get that virus from Priscilla when we need it?"

"Exactly. Only Priscilla is beginning to catch on that the needle stick means she's going to feel lousy in several hours and she doesn't like it too much."

"It sounds very simple," I replied.

A shadow crossed his face. "Well, the immunity thing is a worry." He glanced up sharply. "You've been immunized to polio?"

"Of course."

"The only time this has been attempted, several weeks ago, on a young male, absolutely nothing happened. He just zapped the virus and that was it. I'm going to go up a notch with Amy. It worries me."

"Why? Will she get polio?"

"No, but it could be worse. The body has some very violent ways of dealing with unusual immune circumstances. A single peptide molecule on the surface of the wrong cells can generate a terrible response. Things called killer T cells activate and destroy everything in sight. All sorts of severe reactions follow, including toxic shock and organ failure...followed by death." Scheckler looked at me under heavy brows. If he was trying to scare me off, he was getting close. "How about it, Toni? Still interested?"

"Of course." I wasn't feeling nearly as certain as it sounded.

"Then I'm going to start you on some immune-modifying medication." He darted to another cabinet, took down a bottle and counted out four small blue pills.

"And then?"

"In a few days you'll be ready if your T cells tell me they're going to behave themselves."

"What if I get a cold sore?"

Scheckler laughed. "Well," he said, "that's about it, don't you think?" His smugness irritated me. "Well," he asked, "do you want these or not? Make up your mind, Toni. Time is something you can't afford to waste."

"Not quite," I replied.

"Well?" said Scheckler. His repetition of that word was beginning to drive me nuts.

"I want to see Priscilla," I replied.

Scheckler looked surprised. That irritated me even more. "Why are you interested in Priscilla?" he asked. I was treading on scientific turf. Private property.

"I want to see her. I want to know what she's like."

"Well….," Scheckler hesitated.

That did it. "Dr. Scheckler, stop treating anyone with curiosity about what you're doing as some sort of idiot. I want to see Priscilla. I'm concerned she's being used in all of this. That she's a victim, if you want to put it that way."

Scheckler's hostile mask softened and I saw a different man. A little man who was frightened.

"Miss Putnam," he said slowly, "I hope you know how much Priscilla means to me. She's everything in this effort, but more than that, I'm extremely fond of her…I…wouldn't admit that to anyone else…"

"Good," I replied, "now let me see her."

Scheckler motioned for me to follow, marching importantly toward Priscilla' cage, leaving me to struggle around tables and centrifuges and other junk, all of which had hard metal corners. Priscilla watched through thick plexiglass windows. A heavy layer of straw covered the floor of the small room. A jungle gym was bolted to large metal plates in the center. A tractor tire, apparently a toy, lay on the floor.

Priscilla crouched in one corner, a large compact animal with a short trunk and very long arms and legs, covered with reddish hair. "She is a late adolescent," said Scheckler. "About two hundred fifty pounds. Very pleasant, really. She was raised with humans in Borneo. Her mother was shot by poachers when she was six weeks old."

"I want to go in there," I said.

"Aren't you afraid? She's a very powerful animal," cautioned Scheckler.

"Of course I'm afraid," I replied. He started to turn away. I repeated, "I want to go in there." Aaron Scheckler hesitated, reached over to a peg, snatched off a set of keys and opened the door to the room.

Priscilla slithered toward me on all fours, throwing huge bunches of straw behind her. She grasped the handles of the wheelchair, rising up until her face pressed close and I could smell every breath. Banana and peppermint. She wrinkled her brow then pulled back her lips, displaying enormous canine teeth jutting beyond four-inch incisors. She inched one hand slowly along the shiny chrome arm of the wheelchair. Her head tilted to one side as she concentrated on the sensation of the cold metal. She reached down and ran a blackened finger along the stainless steel footrest. Her light brown eyes returned to my face.

"And so, Priscilla," I asked her, "are you safe-keeping my tiny messengers for me?" I reached out and touched the side of her face.

She realized I was paralyzed. She concentrated on my limp legs, whatever else interested her, my earing, the black braided hair; she returned to the legs, finally running her hand along one and then the other, pushing down into the softened flesh of my thigh with a huge thumb. She turned so suddenly she startled me, hurtling at the jungle gym, swinging swiftly upward, arm over powerful arm, looping back and forth in a frenzy of energy. She then scurried to a back corner, hunched down and watched Aaron Scheckler open the door for me.

"You must promise me," I said to him as I wheeled past, "that you will not do anything to hurt Priscilla on my account." My voice was trembling. I couldn't understand why I was fighting to keep from crying. "I don't want to walk at her expense," I said finally.

"Toni," said Scheckler, "I wouldn't harm Priscilla. She knows that."

Scheckler bent over the sink, filling a small paper cup with water. He brought it to me extending a palm holding the four blue pills. "Do you want these or not?" he asked.

I took the cup and swallowed down the pills. "You don't know what any of the tests are going to show," I said. Why did he always irritate me?

"Putnam," he said, again, as if evening a score of some kind, "you're as healthy as a horse. And besides, as I said, you're very short on time."

TWO REPORTERS

Two students separated from a small group and sprinted to catch me as I pushed hard along the heavily shaded sidewalk leading to Wilson Hall. They were a good looking pair...a slender black girl, tall and leggy, undoubtedly a track star...and a tow-headed boy, also in running shorts and an Ohio University gym shirt. I felt a twinge of jealousy looking at two healthy pairs of legs.

"Hi," greeted the girl, "I'm Glenna Curtis, this is Steve Brody. We're reporters."

"No reporters," I said, not too pleasantly.

"Oh, not *real* reporters," argued Glenna, "The Post. The campus paper. One of the best journalism schools in the country. Did you know that?"

She was a reporter all right. Never stop except on a question.

"You look more like the local track team," I replied.

"We're part of that too, took off from practice to interview an Olympian," Glenna replied. Her expression was very bland, but I could see she knew she was going to get her interview. Anything other than flat rejection equals acceptance. She knew she had made a kill.

I rolled from the sidewalk over the bumpy roots of an ancient sugar maple and turned to face them. "Fire away," I said. Actually I liked them. They were so delighted with themselves.

Brody pulled a beat-up note pad from somewhere. He must have kept the thing in the back of his jock strap. He fished a stub of pencil out of the notebook and wet the tip with his tongue. Ernest Hemingway in the flesh. "We know all about your accident," he volunteered. Brody had a long way to go as a reporter. Glenna flashed him a furious glance.

"Can you tell us about your treatment?" she asked.

"You should discuss that with Dr. Scheckler."

Glenna shrugged as she looked across at the laboratory building. "He lost me in ten seconds," she admitted, "after I spent four hours the night before studying the biology textbook. Something about messenger genes, right?"

"If you understand that, Glenna, you're way ahead of me." We both laughed.

"Our track coach brought in a tape of your Olympic run," said Brody. "He said the Harvard track coach was responsible for your training…he was the one who got you in shape to win."

"That was the Olympic ski coach's idea, not mine," I said, hoping the irritation didn't show. Glenna wasn't fooled.

"Well, did the Harvard track coach train you or not?" persisted Brody.

I decided…screw it. "Right," I replied, "Coach Pearce is phenomenal. I owe everything to the Harvard Athletic Department and Coach Pearce. You can quote me."

Glenna smiled and rubbed the side of her nose with a slender finger. Like we did as kids when we knew someone was blowing smoke. Good reporter vibes.

"Why don't you come to some of our classes while you're waiting for…whatever it is," she asked, "give you something to do. How about Monday? I'll square it with the prof."

"I may do that," I replied. I started to push off.

"At least you were hurt doing something you liked," said Brody, trying once more. "Not shot in the woods like a stupid animal."

"What?" I asked. Glenna glared again at Brody. "What are you talking about?" I repeated.

"Yoder…the other one…" stammered Brody, "got shot off a stump in the woods."

I faced them both. "You better tell me," I said.

Glenna crouched down to my eye level, resting on her heels, holding the arm of my wheelchair. "Amy Yoder lives way down in the hills," she began.

"I know that."

"She practically lived in the woods. She'd wander around in the woods, in good weather sometimes for days at a time. Lived off of berries and roots and things…no kidding. We talked to her. She claims she can speak to the birds and animals. She claims they trust her and come up to her."

"Then she got shot," blurted Brody. The way he jumped around made me I wonder if Brody had missed his morning dose of Ritalin.

Glenna nodded in agreement. "During the turkey season a month ago a hunter crept up on her…in that brown dress and all…and he shot her…mistaking her for a turkey. That's why she's paralyzed."

"Good God." I felt my stomach turn over.

"Yeah," added Brody, "a lawyer from Dayton. Creeping around in a crazy camouflage suit like some commando. Walked away scot free. Offered to pay the medical bills. That's it."

"That won't be 'it' when the lawsuit hits him," I replied.

"Not so," said Glenna, "Amy forgives him. It was an accident. She claims it was meant to happen."

"Meant to happen?" I couldn't believe my ears. I wanted to talk to Amy. "I have to go," I said.

"Hey," said Brody, "at least I'm good for something...how about the old Pony Express?" With that he seized the wheelchair from behind and I had the fastest ride to the dormitory ever recorded.

And who was standing big as life in the archway to the dorm rooms? None other than Vincent Antonelli, looking proud of himself, hands on hips and a big-toothed smile.

"Hey, wow!" said Glenna to Brody as we charged up, "who's the poster boy?"

Brody and Vincent glared at each other as we screeched to a halt. Vince wore a crimson sweatshirt featuring Oliver Wendell Holmes and an inscription below which asked, 'What is it about the IVY LEAGUE that you don't understand?' Just great, I thought.

"Vince!" I exclaimed, "what's happening?"

"Your sainted mother, Toni, ordered in a friendly pit bull to watch out for you." Vincent flashed a meaningful glance at Brody. "At least she told the Dean something like that, he called me in and told me to get lost in Ohio. Only a short jet flight, and three more hours into the wilderness and here I am."

"These are a couple of reporters," I explained. "Glenna Curtis and Steve Brody." They all nodded to one another.

"It's not wilderness," said Brody. He was not in a good mood.

"C'mon, Steve, let's split," said Glenna. She looked Vincent over carefully. "You want to work out, Antonelli, we may not be Ivy League, but we can show you the running path. Protect you from the Indians."

"I'll look you up," promised Vincent, looking puzzled, like he was wondering if he had offended someone.

As soon as we were alone he bent down over the wheelchair, pulled me up to his chest and kissed me hard.

"I missed you a lot," he said.

I have to admit there isn't anybody like Vincent Antonelli to make me feel whole again. I could feel my nipples rubbing my shirt as he squeezed me. I wanted to feel his hands on my bare skin. Where Antonelli was concerned, I was a quick turn-on.

"You ok?" he asked.

"I'm fine." I decided to skip the part about a horrible nightmare and sitting up for two hours afterwards watching the road from the motel window looking for that skinny creep. "Where're you staying?"

"Same place as Scheckler. Within walking distance of his new lab in the Engineering Quad. I'm supposed to keep track of him, remember?"

"Vince, I need to have a long talk with my roommate."

"Right now? How about the two of us? Why not us?"

"She's a scared kid from back in these hills. I'm not sure she has any idea what she's letting herself in for."

"She didn't look too scared to me, Toni. I was up there looking for you and she started in with some nonsense that sounded like cult talk to me. Where's her parents anyway?"

"I've no idea."

"Well, who are you? Mother Theresa? Toni, you're not making sense. You know that don't you? You have a full plate deciding what to do with Scheckler. Forget the missionary work."

"I've already done that."

"Done what?"

"Why don't you talk go talk to Scheckler, Vincent. I want to talk to Amy Yoder. Give me an hour and then come up to the dorm room and we'll go get something to eat."

"All *three* of us?"

"Take it easy, Vince," I warned.

We'd been together for less than ten minutes and already we were arguing.

THE WHIP-POOR-WILL'S SONG

When I wheeled into the dormitory room Amy Yoder was at the window watching Vince walk across the campus. She turned toward me, afternoon sunlight glinting from the metal of the wheelchair.

"He was here looking for you," she said. A smile flickered around her lips. "I would want to say he's a handsome man, but I'm not supposed to say things like that." She considered for a moment. "But I will say it because it's true," she decided.

Innocence is about to find wings, I thought. "Don't let *him* hear that, Amy, he has a big head already."

"He really is, though, Miss Putnam. And very nice. He said he knew all about me from talking to Dr. Scheckler before you came here. Is he a doctor too?"

"Just about. His classes finish this week. Apparently he has been excused to come here."

"I'm sure he's a very good doctor. All of them are."

I decided she was serious, so I let that pass. "Amy, how much do you know about what is going to happen to you next week?"

"I'm afraid I don't understand much of it, Miss Putnam," she replied.

"Amy, how old are you?"

"Eighteen."

"That's just two years younger than I am, Amy. Don't you think it would be better if you called me Toni? We're going to be friends, aren't we?"

"We don't first-name strangers until we're invited…Toni," she replied.

"Why am I a 'stranger', Amy?"

She wheeled over to me, moving her chair beside mine so we faced one another. She took my hand where it rested on the rim and held it in hers.

"Toni," she began hesitantly, "this is the largest town I've ever been in, except for when the ambulance took me to Columbus. We live back on Salt Creek in Vinton County, we're farmers, and we stay to ourselves very much. Our church…we call ourselves Children of God. Outsiders call us Amish, but the Amish would not call us Amish. We're different , we have a school, and only tiny farms; we use the school house for a meeting house and other Amish…"

Amy saw I was not following her. "Oh, Toni, I can't explain." She paused, searching my face, and decided to try again. "Amish are rich. We have nothing. We dress quiet the way Amish dress and only school to the eighth grade…."

She paused again, her face twisting in pain. "What has happened is my fault. Not just my carelessness……"

In the long silence that followed I could hear students laughing and chattering as they passed under the archway of the dorm. "My father is a woodcutter," she said. She spoke so softly I had to lean forward in my wheelchair to hear her.

"My mother…died when I was born. My brothers and sisters in the church tell me my father used to laugh and be a lot of fun before my mother died. Now he never does. And he doesn't seem to want me around. I…can't say why." Amy was watching me like a frightened kitten. She flinched away when I straightened up in the seat. "So I wander in the woods," she continued. "And go to the meetings. In the winter I stay in my room and read my Bible except for the housework." She squeezed my hand as if that would help me understand what she was trying to say.

"The woods," I asked, "that's where you were hurt?"

"Yes. I sat for hours teasing an old tom turkey, you know, gobbling to him," replied Amy. "He was very wary, but was slowly coming closer. He was very jealous, you see." Amy smiled, looking naughty. "And then the hunter shot me off of my stump."

"They hunt turkeys in the *springtime*? When the females are brooding?" I couldn't believe my ears.

"Oh, yes," replied Amy. "The hunters call them up and then shoot them." She paused at my frown. "It was my fault. I should have heard him coming. I wasn't paying attention."

"And then you came here?" I asked. "How did you know to come here?"

"I wouldn't be here except for…the accident. Not even then except that my father said it had to be a sign that Dr. Scheckler came here when he did. A sign that I was supposed to come here and be treated. They talked about it for hours at church, and decided it was a sign. Then my father made them bring me back from Columbus. I was glad he did, I was very frightened there. I don't have to know any more than that. It's all meant to be." She said these last words very slowly.

"You don't know anything about the virus?"

"Do you know the whip-poor-wills that sing to me in the evening from the hollow behind our meeting place? Do you know that they sing only for me?"

"I don't know anything about whip-poor-wills." It was the truth. I had hardly heard of them. "Some bird like an owl," I said finally.

"And I don't know anything about viruses."

"Amy, where *is* your father? Does he agree with all of this? Do you have *anyone* who's looking out for you?"

"My father came and signed the papers. They...my friends...are praying for me. They're with me all the time. But they don't stay in cities. We have only one telephone...in a phone shanty on the county road. You shouldn't worry, Toni, I'm not alone. I'll send a message when I'm cured and my father will fetch me. The one thing I want, I cannot have...I want to listen to my whip-poor-will before I...do whatever it is, but my whip-poor-will doesn't like cities any more than I do, so he must sing to me in my heart."

I was beginning to understand. "How far away is your bird, Amy?"

"Behind our church in the hollow, Toni." She paused, gradually sensing why I was asking. When she was certain she understood her eyes sparkled as they widened in disbelief. Then she laughed. The innocent delighted laugh of a child opening a present.

"Oh, Toni, tomorrow we have service in our church. Would you come? Would you take me there? Afterwards the whip-poor-wills are going to sing, I promise!"

* * *

That evening my mother telephoned. I've never had a reasonable telephone conversation with my mother, going back as far as age eight. Barney said it was because both of us talked and neither one listened. Tonight was no different. First of all she wanted to be certain the bulldog had arrived and was on duty.

"I thought you didn't like Antonelli?" I replied to her question.

"I don't like him," she replied, "but apparently you do. So I asked him to get down there and see to it that you were being properly treated, or whatever it is. What *is* being done, Toni? Your father is beside himself."

"I saw Dr. Scheckler today and he did some blood tests."

"What sort of tests?"

"Something about immune responses of some certain cells." I realized if I called the things 'killer T cells' she would call out the National Guard.

"What does your young doctor have to say about that?"

"He says they're just the thing." A lie. Antonelli didn't know anything about the tests. Or killer T cells either, for that matter.

"I don't like that Dr. Scheckler."

"Mother, you don't know him."

"You know what I'm talking about."

"He's been cold sober ever since he arrived." Another lie, Vincent told me he saw Scheckler heading into a local bar as he was on his way to take us to dinner.

"Are you comfortable? Where are you staying? Not with…."

"Mother, I have a nice roommate. A very religious girl. We're going to her church tomorrow."

I thought that was a solid sure-fire hit. Wrong! There was a very long silence.

"What sort of church?"

"I believe it's called some sort of Amish."

"Do you mean the Pennsylvania Dutch?"

"I guess. Sort of."

"What do you mean, *sort of?*"

"I don't understand the differences between Amy's church, who call themselves 'Children of God', and regular Amish…whatever that is."

Another long silence.

"Toni, you're getting mixed up in some cult."

"Mother, this is a very nice girl. I'm not joining anything."

"People…with your…problem are very vulnerable to cults. *They* know that. Toni, they're very clever."

"Do you mean we cripples, mother?"

"Toni, don't be nasty." She was crying softly. Why did I always have to be such a jerk and treat my mother that way?

"Mother, I'm sorry. Please don't worry. Vincent won't let any cult get me."

"Well, he'd better not. He's not as firm as I would like. I wish Hughes was down there instead. Hughes is much more firm. And besides Hughes is an attorney…or almost."

"Can we talk about something else? How's Barney?"

"Toni, if the slightest thing happens to you, your father is going to have that man drawn and quartered."

I was getting desperate. "Well, how *is* Hughes Lawrence, mother? Has he found a nice Boston girl yet?"

"My friends tell me he's waiting for you to come to your senses. Oh, Toni, how I wish you would give him a call. He could do so much for you. He's such a fine man."

"Perhaps I will, Mother"

"Toni, stay out of that strange church. Don't be tempting the Devil."

"I'll remember that, Mother." On that we said goodbye.

THE MEETING PLACE

We drove into the Appalachian hills on Sunday afternoon. Amy insisted on naming each farm as we passed. The land became poorer and more hilly, there were large areas of scrub and briars and each side road was more narrow and winding. Crop-land disappeared, replaced by scattered shacks, abandoned hulks of old cars, and farm machinery rusted at the edges of snatches of plowed ground and rail fences.

The roads deteriorated to a mixture of gravel and ancient macadam, the last of which dipped through a creek in several places. Vincent looked over and raised his eyebrows, but was smart enough to keep silent.

"That's the Wayne National Forest," said Amy proudly, sweeping her arm broadly over the hills. "I've walked miles of it in the evenings after chores were over, sometimes I didn't come home at all. My father was very understanding."

Since I already knew all of that, I assumed this was for Vince's benefit. "Aren't you afraid?" I asked.

"Oh, if I hear 'coon dogs I just make sure I lose them," she replied. "They aren't nearly as smart as people think they are. Neither are the hunters."

She shifted over to the other side of the van, steadied the wheelchair by holding the edge of the cot and pointed toward a tangle of brush and small trees.

"There's *seng* in there," she said, "a *seng* patch. They pay good money for *seng*. I know where a lot of it is, but I don't tell. I don't want it torn out."

"Genseng," supplied Vincent, apparently assuming I needed a second tour guide. "The root is supposed to be medicinal. The Chinese are nuts about it. Supposed to prolong life…and prolong a lot of other things, too." Vincent was watching Amy like she was a piece of chocolate cake. I think it was the black bonnet. As if he had never seen one of those before.

*   *   *

The meeting house was a small white frame building with a wide front porch and steep steps leading up to it. The leafy yard enclosing the building was filled with buggies and patient horses, many of which munched contentedly from canvas bags fitting over their noses and strapped behind the ears.

The van's grid lowered Amy and she was surrounded by well wishers, although very subdued in manner, and when the grid returned and eventually delivered me, they peered closely while I was introduced. They wore brown or black dresses, and cheerful faces framed by a tightly formed bun of hair beneath the bonnet, smiling shyly. Several volunteered, "Welcome, sister."

Men who sauntered over wore denim coveralls or dark suits, most were bearded except for a few husky young men who were beardless. They were more interested in Vincent as he emerged from the passenger's side than they were in Amy or me. I was relieved that Vince had abandoned the Oliver Wendell Holmes sweatshirt for a pin-striped oxford shirt and a tennis sweater but he still looked very strange shaking hands with these farmers in their broad-brimmed black hats.

When they tried to make conversation, Vince answered awkwardly. He was not comfortable, which puzzled me; his usual approach to strangers is that of a traveling salesman, or if he is really feeling his oats, a long-lost relative.

"Don't you like these people?" I asked him when I had a chance. "You look like you're seeing ghosts."

"You haven't seen that old man glaring at you from beyond that last buggy, Toni," he replied. "I'll bet you ten bucks that's Amy's old man, and you're not exactly welcome."

I looked quickly, and saw Jakob Yoder for the first time. A heavy stocky man like all of the others, dressed as they were, but set apart by fierce eyes that burned at me like hot coals in a dying grate. He quickly looked away. I shivered. I half expected to see that naked skinny white escaped prisoner running between the huge trees that shaded him.

A bell tolled softly in the tiny tower atop the ridge of the meeting house. Several of the women motioned to Amy. We were pushed over the rough ground to the porch. Two husky young men grasped each of my wheels and walked up the flight of steps as if I was a feather. Two others did the same for Amy.

"We built it sort of high because of the creek," explained one of my bearers, looking at me with soft brown eyes. His shoulders stretched the fabric of his coat. He was very broad and very square.

I glanced back at Vincent. "Come on," I said, beckoning with my hand.

"I'm staying out here, Toni," he said. "I'll be out here. Don't worry about me. I belong out here with the horses." The others moved on into the building as if they didn't see or hear him.

✶   ✶   ✶

The interior of the meeting house was painted white with a row of small windows along the sides and filled with dark benches arranged in a deep semi-circle. It had the clean smell of strong soap, the pine flooring was unvarnished and very smooth; a holystone and a mop in the corner explained its spotless appearance. I maneuvered my wheelchair against the back wall. Amy went forward, surrounded by chattering 'sisters', her face suffused a bright pink with excitement and happiness. They settled in, the buzzing of conversation diminished to silence.

The sound of crows and chickadees and the soft crunching of the feeding horses filtered from the open windows. The silence remained unbroken for over thirty minutes. Then they started to sing softly, there was no organ or other instrument, or any evidence of a leader. It was a pleasant sound, perfectly on key but with endless repetition. The tune was sad and the words were in German. It went on for another very long time. Finally one of the men stood up and began to speak, none of which I understood. The monotone went on and on, gradually fading as I dozed.

It was the silence which startled me awake. The afternoon sun was much lower on the windows.

When a man spoke, I jumped. It was Jakob Yoder. His voice was harsh and as I startled awake he was pointing at Amy, who was now in the middle of the semicircle of benches, crying softly.

"There *had to be sin!*" thundered Yoder. The thick finger wavered several inches from his daughter. "*Find it!*" he demanded, "and you will walk again! This man who was sent is only a *vessel* and a *tainted one at that*! Find your sin, daughter, and he can cure you! Stay in your conceit and you will live and die in that useless contraption!" His quivering finger hovered over the wheelchair.

He spun around. My God! He was glowering at me! The beard shook from his rage. There was spittle on his lips. I opened my mouth to scream for Antonelli.

"Silence!," he shouted, as if reading my mind. "You will not be harmed! I bear you no ill will." He certainly looked like he did.

"You're so steeped in sin you know nothing else," he accused. "You're lost," he concluded, his voice dropping.

He turned away, his face haggard.

Amy pushed one wheel rim to turn toward us. In the silence she took her time to carefully wipe the corners of her eyes with a tiny handkerchief, then compose herself before she spoke.

"I'm to have a special treatment this week," she said simply. "I've been full of fear. I've asked for comfort, but have not been strong enough to hold on to the comfort I was given." She looked toward me. "A new friend came here two days ago. She's a very strong person, not weak like me. She's shown me what it's like to have the sort of courage God gives to us all if we're strong enough to hold on to it."

Soft murmurs from the rows of benches drowned the buzzing of the flies.

"I'm ready for what comes," continued Amy. "I believe *she* was sent here to give me courage when mine was failing me. I believe she's part of the sign. She's part of the meaning of all of this."

Amy jabbed at the wheel rim to turn back toward her father who was hunched down on a front bench, his face hidden.

"I know I've sinned," she said to him. "I know it." She tossed her head back from him abruptly. "I'll be forgiven."

Several loud "Amens!"

*   *   *

Sturdy women bustled about under the freshly leafed trees spreading food in abundance. Tables heaped with back meat, chicken, ham, collards, tomatoes, beans; all scooped from huge oven pans or poured from freshly opened mason jars. On an adjoining trestle table rested pies, bread, biscuits, cookies, and small cakes.

Vincent Antonelli was suddenly cheerful. He pitched in with a vengeance. He had a big smear of buttermilk on his upper lip which I told him to wipe off. I was frightened out of my wits and trying to hide it. Amy bounced over the rough ground toward the table where Vince was stuffing himself. She looked radiantly happy. I couldn't believe it. The trusting expression made me feel like a witch.

"Amy," I said, "we're not on the same page. Do you have any idea what I'm trying to tell you?"

She smiled knowingly. "Sister Toni," she said, "you're embarrassed by what I said. I'm sorry. But I told the truth. It's our way. And you must not be afraid of my father. It's his way of getting in touch with God. He would never harm you. But…" she hesitated, "he also thinks he's speaking the truth."

I felt like telling her she wasn't my sister. I wanted to tell her I had no idea whether I was going to let Aaron Scheckler infect me with his virus or not.

"Amy…you need to think carefully about this…" was all I came up with.

"I've thought about it."

"Perhaps you should wait a bit."

"I was told if I don't make up my mind quickly my chance for it to work might be lost."

"What if you waited just…until you see what I decide to do?"

"No."

"I want to speak to your father, Amy."

"Over there." She nodded toward a group of men talking beside one of the wagons.

"Vince," I said irritably, would you please finish that plate and take me over there?"

I was not going get close to Jakob Yoder without Vince, and I wasn't going to be struggling across tree roots and gravel while Jakob Yoder watched me labor for what he probably thought was my just punishment.

As we approached, the group of men regarded me warily. As if horns might sprout out of my forehead.

I did my best to explain to Jacob Yoder what I knew about the messenger virus, the orangutan, all of it. I should've saved my breath. All I got was another lecture. Jakob Yoder heard me out with infuriating patience, then spoke very slowly. As far as he was concerned he was talking to a moron.

"This was meant to be," he said simply. "We believe when something this terrible happens to an innocent...someone as innocent as Amy...it has to have meaning. And it doesn't happen without *sin*. If we repent we are sent a sign. I received the sign. Not the girl, the sign was sent to *me*. I'm only trying to help her."

"As for you," he raised his eyebrows, "I spoke the truth where only the truth can be spoken. I meant to help, not harm." He glanced at the other men as he puffed up. And he wasn't finished.

"We call it a sign," he repeated. "Do you really think, sister, that this famous doctor just happened here? Here of all places? A famous doctor in this backwash? Here with a cure? We believe it's no accident, sister. God does not play with us!" His eyes flashed at me, but when he saw me flinch, he reached out and pressed on my hand where it rested on the rim of my wheelchair. I expected it to catch fire.

"Don't be angry with me, sister," he said. "Let us follow our way, and you follow yours." He turned away. Amy wheeled after him, stopped him, and they talked; he leaned down over her chair, his huge hand on her shoulder. Then he walked away. Amy rolled back to me, smiling again.

"Come on, Toni," she said, "don't look so fierce." She looked up into the evening sky.

"It's time to go up the hollow to see if my whip-poor-will is willing to sing for us," she said cheerfully.

The setting sun found us laboring along a sandy pathway, most of it uphill while Antonelli, who at least could have pushed, had declined. I think he had hopes of another dessert while the women were packing up.

At the top of the hollow we entered the thick forest and pressed on to the edge of a huge crystalline spring. We were exhausted and sweating. We stared at each other, thinking of the same thing.

"I want to tell you something, Toni," said Amy, her voice shaking. "I've never told anyone." She reached down and removed her slippers, flipped up her footrests and adjusted her helpless legs down into a patch of watercress at the edge of the swirling cold water.

"When I, you know, started to become a woman," she began, "my father turned very strange. He came into the kitchen at night when I was bathing in the galvanized tub. At first he acted surprised. Like he didn't hear me heating the water, but then...he would just come and stay. He...always talked about my mother." Amy looked at me with stricken eyes. "I...never knew my mother. Then...he would want to touch me." She buried her face in her hands. "One night he snatched me up out of the tub, all wet and dripping, I started crying and screaming, screaming for my mother to help me!"

"Amy," I said.

"No!," she shouted, "I have to tell you. Don't you understand?" She started sobbing. "He swore and threw me down and then ordered me outside. It was cold outside! I went into the barn with the cow to keep warm. In the morning there was a pile of clothes in the manger. It was a week before I went back to the house. I go to the creek when I want to bathe. In the winter I don't bathe at all."

"Amy, he's wrong. Don't you understand? *Can't* you understand?" My voice was gritty with anger.

"Don't *say* that. He's my *father*. He expected me to take my mother's place. He's a *man*. That's my sin, Toni, I know it! I was prideful! I was thinking of *myself*! What happened was my punishment. And if you don't believe that, you're sinful the way he said!"

I wanted to pick her up, throw her in the spring and tell her she was now forgiven. Even Jakob should appreciate that. As it was I sat and watched the water swirl from the pure deep depths, reflecting the orange and yellows of the setting sun. Amy searched for my hand, her's felt as cold as ice water. But the desperate grip told me she was drowning in misery.

The soft trill of a night bird sounded in the depths of the darkening ravine. Sad notes rising rapidly, almost frantically on to a fourth or fifth repetition…*whip-poor-will….whip-poor-will…whip-poor-will…whip-poor-will!* There was silence until answered by another call deeper in the woods. Amy lifted her head and listened. The first bird repeated, then a return, then tumbling into one another. Then silence.

"What do they look like?" I asked.

"Oh, Toni, you never see them," said Amy. "The Indians believed they were spirits of loved ones singing in the night. You're not supposed to see them!"

"They sound sad."

"Oh no. They're trying to tell you there's life all around us, even if unseen. They try to comfort someone who is lonely. They say 'never be lonely'."

"Well, Amy, I do like them," I replied.

"They always sing for me, Toni."

"They sing that you are forgiven, Amy." If everyone around here was telling whoppers, why not me?

Amy smiled knowingly. "You're my friend, Toni," she whispered. "Even if you're a sinner" She giggled like it was a joke. What was going *on*, I wondered. What is it with these people, some sort of game? If so, count me out.

But Amy was listening for another call. When it came, she nodded her head, satisfied. "And I know you love me," she said. I couldn't tell in the dim twilight if she was talking to me or the bird.

"When you hear a whip-poor-will you must always think of me." So, she was talking to me. What a strange thing to say. As if she could see what I could not.

THE VIRUS STRIKES

The following morning the laboratory appeared to be unchanged. The glassware remained where it had been carefully placed. Scheckler, for all of his personal appearance, was extremely fussy about his laboratory. A white vapor hovered over the container of dry ice, the sound of the centrifuge filled the room with soft hum.

But there were significant differences, Scheckler was freshly scrubbed and alert, a healthy pink replaced the usual sallowness of his skin, and he was, if anything, more intense. Black eyes snapped behind thick brows and his motions were quick and purposeful. He bent over Priscilla who was lying along the back wall of her cage, her nose dripping. She obviously did not feel well. Scheckler coaxed her to drink from a cup, which she did in small sips while gazing at him with dislike. Scheckler stood up, waving us toward his desk at the front of the room. He hurried out to us after carefully closing the thick steel door. "Nothing like beta interferone to knock a virus," he said cheerfully. "Priscilla will be feeling much better by noon, and will be over this in one or two days." He waved his hand toward the centrifuge humming in the corner. "We'll have our prepared sample in several minutes." He reached over and took Amy's pulse. "You ready for this?" he asked.

Amy looked at me and then at Scheckler. She held her lips tightly compressed, her chin trembled slightly. She nodded her head at the doctor.

"Amy," I said, "you don't have to do this if you don't want to do it. There's no reason to go ahead if you don't wish to do this."

Scheckler looked irritated, but after a slight hesitation said, "I agree completely, Amy. It's not too late to decide not to do this."

"No," said Amy. "I want to do this." Her voice sank to a whisper. "It's meant to be."

The centrifuge clicked off and there was only the whirring as it slowed and finally stopped with a second sharp click. Scheckler hurried over to it, removed a long glass tube and took it over to a refrigerator. He opened the door, withdrew a plastic jug of orange juice. It seemed very much out of place. He mixed the liquid contents of the tube with the juice and brought it over to Amy. As he extended it his hand shook slightly. "Well, Amy," he said, "with all my heart I hope this will enable you to walk again. I've done all I can, the rest is up to you and our friendly virus."

Amy glanced at me, then took the glass and drank it down. Scheckler shrugged his shoulders. "That's all there is to it. Stay in the dormitory, Toni will be with you. You'll get a fever and then an illness very much like the flu. It will last about four days. I'll look in every few hours. There will be blood tests every day, but I'll come and get them until you're feeling well again."

*   *   *

We wheeled side-by-side along the blacktop sidewalk toward the dormitory, groups of students parting as they drifted past, most of them waved or called us by name. Amy was smiling and seemed relaxed. Once we were in the room she admitted she was tired. I turned down her bed and steadied her wheelchair with mine and half lifted her as she struggled into bed. Once covered with a light blanket she smiled at me and finally dozed off. She had removed her bonnet and her beautiful dark brown hair spilled over the pillow. She looked very much at peace with herself.

I sat by the dorm window in my wheelchair watching the students hurry back and forth, many serious, a few with worried expressions. I wondered what could possibly be concerning them on such a beautiful day. Others were laughing and fooling around; young strong legs, solid bodies, oblivious of their fantastic good fortune.

I saw Vincent Antonelli jogging across the commons with Glenna Curtiss. He had scrounged an Ohio University track uniform and he looked good, all solid muscle and a deep tan. But if he looked like a solid runner, she looked like a gazelle. She was pacing him carefully, and as they passed under the archway of the dorm they waved at me. I could tell from the look on Glenna's face that she was going to run his ass off when she got him down on the bicycle path along the Hocking River. A woman after my own heart.

*   *   *

It was noon when Vincent tapped on the door to our room. He had showered and was wearing jeans and a Harvard tee shirt, but looked like he had been dragged in by a mule.

He flopped in a chair. "My God, Toni," he said, "she nearly killed me."

"Serves you right wearing that Ivy League stuff around here."

"She said about as much. But you know how it is, Toni, never show the white feather and all that."

"Pearce would be real proud of you." The last time I had thought about my favorite track coach I was cracking the ribs of that skinny hitch-hiker.

"What's wrong, Toni?" Vince asked. "You look like you've just seen a ghost." When I shrugged, he continued. "Pearce stopped me once at Soldier's Field and told me I run like a duck."

"I imagine most hockey jocks do."

But Vincent was looking at Amy. He jumped up and ran to her, placing his hand lightly on her forehead.

"Jesus, Toni," he said, "she's burning up!" he exclaimed.

"Scheckler said she would get a fever," I replied, but the look on his face sent a jolt of fear through my stomach.

"I'm going to get him," he snapped, and he bolted out the door.

When I looked back, Amy was sitting upright, swaying on the edge of the bed. She stared wildly at me. She was wheezing and trying to cough. She looked down at her legs. Then she slid off of the bed onto her legs, staggered and pitched forward. I was just able to roll under her so that she fell on me and we then rolled crazily back across the room and crashed into a desk. I eased her down onto the floor, shouting for help. Her skin was dry as parchment and hot as summer pavement. I had never felt such hot skin.

Students rushed in from adjacent rooms and lifted Amy onto her bed. Blood ran from her nose. There were shouts and screams, and various first-aid attempts, but very soon Aaron Scheckler was there, feeling her pulse, opening a small bag with trembling hands and wrapping on a blood pressure cuff. He watched the dial as he released the cuff, Vincent leaning over his shoulder. They looked at each other. Scheckler grabbed the telephone on the desk and dialed.

"Dean Henderson," he shouted. There was a pause. "Dean," said Scheckler, "the Yoder woman is having a toxic immune reaction. We need to get her to a tertiary center. Is that Ohio State?" He paused. "OK, get an ambulance over here!"

Scheckler twisted toward us, his gray face streaming sweat. "Will you ride with us, Antonelli?" he asked. Scheckler was shaking like a leaf.

"Certainly. Do they have anything other than fluids and oxygen?"

"Not until we get her in a unit." He paused to think. "I don't know. I don't know. He waved long slender fingers in the air. "She's going to start to bleed. See if we can get some platelets somewhere."

The ambulance arrived. I managed to crowd into an elevator with the help of several students.

As I wheeled into the sunshine Vincent ran up to me. "She won't leave without speaking to you, Toni," he said. "Hurry up."

They slid the gurney back out of the ambulance so we could lean close together. Amy's left eye was a bloody bulge where the white should have been. She wheezed as I put my ear close to her. "Toni," she said, "this is my fault." She paused trying to get breath. "I lied. I was never immunized against polio. We...don't believe it's God's way. But I wanted the medicine so I lied to the doctor."

"Oh, Amy!" I was choking back tears.

Amy pleaded with me. "Toni, I want to go home. Don't let them take me *back there to that big hospital.* They will do things to me. Tubes and everything. I don't want that. I want to go home where I belong!" She sobbed and clutched my hand.

Scheckler was beside me, urging me to get out of the way.

"She wants to go back to her home," I said.

"Are you insane?" snapped Scheckler, "She needs a critical care unit!"

"You'd better get on a telephone and talk to Jakob Yoder or you're going to be looking into the wrong end of a shotgun," I warned.

"They don't believe in telephones," snapped Scheckler. He was fighting for an excuse.

"They have a shanty on some road corner just for things like this, and you better find him," I repeated. "I think he will tell you to bring her home." Scheckler swore and clambered into the ambulance.

"I'm going with her," Vincent Antonelli said at my side. I turned and stared at him. He nodded at me grimly. "I'm going with her, wherever it is," he announced. He jumped into the back of the ambulance. A medic moved over to make room for him.

As they slammed the back door I heard Amy shouting...as loud a noise as I had ever hear her make. "Don't quit Toni," cried the shrill voice. "Not because I lied! Don't stop."

The ambulance screeched out of the parking lot. I was left in the falling darkness with a circle of students watching me, some of them crying. Several tried to say something, but words failed. They stood mutely looking at the wheelchair and then at me.

SUICIDE WATCH

I parked my wheelchair at the dorm windowsill and watched students crossing the commons in the fading twilight. They were laughing and talking, holding one another, others teasing and play-fighting; gusts of cold evening wind whipped at skirts and jackets.

High cumulus clouds caught the setting sun on their highest peaks. I tried to trace where they might be racing against time in the black shadows of the valleys; dying Amy, Scheckler, the driver, the two medics, and Vince. What was happening? Did they rush toward Columbus? If so, perhaps they were there. Or were they commanded to take Amy home? Would they do that? She told me her cabin was tiny. What would they do then? What was happening? I twisted painfully in the chair. It might as well have been a cage.

A group of students gathered in the archway below me. They held candles and kept retreating to a corner to relight them, trying to make a tight circle to shut out gusts of wind. Some looked up and waved, some were praying. One boy was passing out cans of beer.

I stared into the darkness as candles flickered and failed, someone finally lit a kerosene lantern. I fell asleep slumped in the chair.

The cold jarred me awake, frigid torrents of wind flapping curtains behind me like the wings of a gigantic black bat. I clutched my throat, certain I felt skinny hands circling it as I smelled the stinking dead unwashed smell of his grimy white body. I threshed about in the darkness to throw him off, rocking crazily across the room and slamming into the wall before coming to my senses. I wheeled down to the bathroom and emptied the urine bag. By my watch it was 2:30 A.M. I returned warily to the room, peering into every dark corner, forcing myself to turn my back to the empty blackness and crawl up into the bed. I could make out the pale outline of Amy's pillow across the night stand. If she'd been there I would have crawled in beside her and asked her to hold me. But Amy was not there. Amy was somewhere, as alone as I was, and fighting to breathe. I pulled covers over me and shivered. I was too exhausted to get up and close the window.

∗ ∗ ∗

Vincent called at 5:30. Faint early light glistened on droplets of mist on the window screen.

"She's gone, Toni," he said. My throat tightened in the silence that followed.

"It was awful," he continued. "She never complained. We put her in her bed, she was bleeding and gasping for breath, she did let us give her some oxygen, but waved everything else away. It went on for *hours*. Scheckler was frantic. They finally had to take him away...to somewhere else. He was shouting, frothing at the mouth, then sobbing. Amy used her strength trying to comfort him...they...had to take him away," he repeated. I heard him take a deep breath.

"They let me stay beside her," he continued, his voice breaking. "That's what Amy wanted. So they let me sit at her head. I put cold compresses on her forehead...it was all I could think of to do..." Vince's voice trailed off and I heard rustling sounds as he covered the mouthpiece with his hand. When he finally spoke his voice was more composed.

"Even in the middle of all that mess, she looked up at me once with those horrible bloody eyes and said, 'You should love her, you know. Toni would be very good for you.'"

"Vince, get hold of yourself. You're rambling," I said sternly.

"Toni, I have to talk to you. Henderson's sending a van out for us. He wants me to stay with Scheckler...I mean in his room at the motel...I think they're afraid he might...do something. Henderson told me if they can't settle him down they're going to put him in O'Bleness Hospital. Before I do any of that I have to talk with you. I don't know if I'm cut out for any of this. Do you know what I mean?"

"I think you're worn out, Vince. And I think you've had a very bad experience."

"Toni, I've been around a lot of death in the last four years. You know, over at Children's with the tiny bald kids on chemo and all. But never anything like this. At the hospital, no matter how bad it is there's always hope. Or at least someone who knows what they're doing."

There was more rustling and a pause. "But this! That girl looking at me and trying to comfort me! The others, one sitting across from me holding Amy's hand. Old Jakob stomping in and out and glaring at me. I tried to give him my place, but as he started to sit down, Amy screamed and clutched for me and Jakob ran out of the room like a whipped dog!"

"I know how she felt, Vince. It's not any of your doing."

"I still need to see you, Toni. I think we need to get out of this place before something else happens."

"I'll be here, Vincent, when you get here."

∗   ∗   ∗

He came at 1:30, walking across the commons, looking disheveled; when he faced me in the room there was heavy black stubble of beard and reddened eyes from lack of sleep.

"I knew something like this was going to happen," he said as he threw himself into the chair beside me at the window. "I sensed it. Too many loose ends." He rubbed his eyes with his fingertips. "Well, anyway, it's all over."

"What do you mean?" I asked.

He pulled his hands down onto his cheeks, staring at me. "What do you think I mean? The laboratory, Priscilla, all of it. Scheckler's finished, admits as much. Henderson has been great. He told Scheckler over and over there was a place for him on the faculty, how much the students admired him, how much they needed someone with his abilities. He went on and on. Scheckler just kept shaking his head. I think Henderson is smart to put me on a suicide watch."

"So why does Scheckler have to give up?"

"Toni, are you crazy? Do you think *anyone* would consider continuing this nutty business?"

"That isn't what you said before you had me come out here. You said a lot of people thought Scheckler was making a lot of sense."

"Toni, you have to give this up. Your father was right. I'm as responsible as anyone for all of this. I'm taking you back to Boston just as soon as the Dean says I'm not needed around here."

"Oh?"

"Go ahead and get pissed. We're going. Your father is probably going to meet me with a shotgun anyway, not that I would blame him."

"I thought I might have something to say about all of this."

Vincent paused, deep in thought. "Toni, I'm really beat," he said. "Why don't you come over to Scheckler's room with me? I need a shower, and I've got to have a couple of hour's sleep. You can baby-sit. Let Scheckler convince you this is all over. I promise after I have a quick nap, you can start packing up. If we do it this way I won't have to worry about falling asleep while I sit there watching him. When Henderson turns us loose, I'm going to sleep all the way back to Boston."

Vince insisted on pushing me across the commons. Like he was my wet-nurse. Made me furious. In front of the motel room two half-filled whiskey bottles were trashed in a battered wastebasket. Dr. Scheckler sat on one unmade twin bed, Dean Henderson sat at a small writing desk.

"Who's throwing out good whiskey?" I asked. Henderson nodded toward Scheckler.

"That's over," answered Scheckler. "At least I can do that much." His eye sockets were two dark holes, the skin beneath was bluish. The corner of his mouth was twitching. Scheckler covered it with his hand.

Dean Henderson relaxed as Vince crossed the room toward the shower. "Remember what I've said, Aaron," he said firmly. "We are behind you. We both know medicine has its tragedies. As far back as smallpox vaccination, for that matter. The faculty will be behind you as well." Vince was right. Henderson was quite a man. Scheckler seemed to take no notice.

When I sat down on the empty bed, the Dean smiled, stood up from his chair, buttoned his raincoat and hurried out the front door, slamming it behind him. I heard the shower start.

"So when do we get on with this?" I asked Scheckler. I caught a flash of the old anger. Then he shook his head sadly. "How I wish we could, Toni," he replied.

"Well?"

"Toni, it's over for me. For us. Someone will pick up on it, believe me. But I'm sorry to say, it will be much too late for you. You need to plan a new life. I've no doubt you will do that."

He rubbed his forehead. "Do you mind if I lie down? I've taken a heavy dose of sleeping pills…Henderson watched me, don't worry." He smiled his crooked smile.

He lay back on the bed. "Jakob Yoder was a madman. They had to pull him off me. He shouted he would find me and burn me!"

"But what about Priscilla and the virus?" I asked.

"Oh," he replied sleepily, Priscilla will go up to the Columbus zoo. It's one of the best primate zoos in the world, you know."

"But what about...?" I stopped. Aaron Scheckler was deep in exhausted sleep. I looked over at the dresser beside the bed. His keys and wallet lay on top. I guided the wheelchair quietly to the dresser, stopped to listen to the rushing of the shower in the bathroom, looked the keys over, peeled several off of the ring, and slipped silently out of the room.

ORANGUTAN RAGE

I tried the keys on the laboratory door. The second one worked. I leaned heavily against the thick metal door, fighting for traction. Slowly it opened to the gloom of the laboratory. Priscilla stirred in her room, moving back and forth, a huge hairy dark shadow under the dim light over her jungle gym. She loped to plexiglass windows, massive shoulder muscles tensed as she raised her arms high on the thick pane, flexing huge black fingers. Like I was a toy and she wanted to play.

I yanked out the chair at Scheckler's desk, threw it aside and maneuvered myself into the knee hole. I snapped on the halogen lamp, blinding myself momentarily, finally found his notebook and studied the scrawled pages. My medical data was on a sheet tucked behind the last page. The more I studied it, the less it made any sense. Several texts lay to one side, I opened them and flipped through them. I studied the clipboard chart with my name on it, read my history, the notes on my physical examination and a page of neurology notes which made no sense.

I wheeled to the cabinet beside the centrifuge, opened it, took down the familiar bottle and poured four blue pills into my palm. There was a tiny white inscription on each one which looked like a skull but on close inspection were two superimposed letters. I rolled them around, fighting nausea and fear; finally used my free hand to wobble over to the sink. I stretched up for a gleaming beaker, filled it with water and tossed down the pills, gagging on the last one, but finally forcing it down. I imagined I could feel each pill burn all the way into my stomach.

I forced myself to roll my wheelchair back to the windows of Priscilla's room. She charged about the cage, pounded heavily on the window with both fists, then seized the huge tractor tire from the hay and threw it across the room where it thudded against the wall and rolled crazily to a stop.

I opened the small refrigerator beside her door. A single 2 cc. syringe lay on a shelf, filled with a pale pink liquid. Beside the syringe was the half empty gallon jug of orange juice. On the shelf below lay four bananas and several oranges and beside them a cardboard box containing rolls of Mentos. I peeled two oranges and grabbed a roll of the candy.

I carefully picked up the syringe with its needle and cap,, than selected several bananas, the oranges and a roll of the candy, piling it all carefully between my legs. I stretched up to snatch the key from its peg and used it to open the heavy steel door to her room.

Priscilla slithered to me, stabbing a quick black hand between my legs, then filled her massive mouth with the oranges. She grimaced, showing enormous white teeth in the dimness and petulantly splattered the bananas against the plexiglass window. Then she expertly peeled the foil from the package of Mentos and tossed in several of the tiny mints. She scrambled to the back wall, clutching the roll of Mentos, pressed her back into the far corner, slowly sliding down onto her haunches. From there she glared at me from under heavy black brows; tiny glistening eyes like sparks in the deep shadows of her face.

I looked at my hands. They shook uncontrollably and had no strength. I pressed them against my face. They seemed as numb as my legs. All I could feel was all-consuming terror.

"I can't do it," I muttered as I waited for some feeling of self-control. All I could see were those glittering eyes.

"I can't." No control or willingness to go to Priscilla came to me. I slammed the door and hung up the key. I picked the syringe out of my lap and threw it onto the shelf of the refrigerator. The door closed softly.

I wheeled aimlessly across the commons, passing students who started to speak, but broke off when they looked closely at me. I know my face was tear-streaked whatever else turned them off. I found myself staring across the parking lot at the van. The hills rose beyond. Somewhere in there they were burying Amy Yoder.

I had lost all of my courage. Everything she was so proud to see in me. I was losing my self-respect. All that had saved me from that nasty murderer was gone. I would be nothing if he ever found me. And I knew some day he would.

It was then I realized I had to go back into those hills. There had to be a way to save myself.

THE WHIP-POOR-WILL'S MESSAGE

The roads were winding and endless. By late afternoon I was lost. It all looked the same. But I was convinced I was getting closer. I pulled alongside a solemn little boy marching along the edge of the dusty road. He wore one of the black Amish hats, only it was gray with thick white dust and frayed at the brim. It pressed down the tops of both ears, flopping them forward which gave him a retarded look. He carried a small spinning rod. When I stopped beside him, he continued walking, forcing me to ease slowly along with him.

"Am I on the road to the meeting house?" I asked.

He puzzled for a moment, then nodded.

"How far away is it?"

"'Bout four mile."

"Thanks." I started to pull ahead.

"Fer what?" I heard him ask behind me.

I slowed while he caught up. "For telling me how to get there," I said. I gave him a friendly smile.

"Lady, you ain't never going to get there. Yer goin' the wrong way," he replied. His face was serious.

"Take the left fork two mile up," he shouted through the cloud of dust as I spun and jerked the van back and forth to turn it around. "Can't miss it."

Once upon the side road I remembered the rest of it. The sun was low when I pulled into the grassy yard before the meeting house. It was empty except for a solitary buggy with a dusty horse standing patiently in the traces. The grass was trampled where others had stood. Crows called from the ravine that ran beyond the building.

Jakob Yoder came out onto the porch of the meeting house and faced me, fists resting on his hips. He wore a shiny black suit, his black beard jutted down from his chin, the hat came nearly to his brows. He looked massive, like a huge piece of black lava. I triggered the door and then the lift, unlatched myself, turned into the back and struggled onto the grid. I took a deep breath and pressed the remote to lower myself to the ground. As I rolled off onto the grass he marched down the steps to meet me.

"She's already buried," he said. His voice was low, trembling, and full of pain. "It's our way."

"I know that, Jakob. I'm sorry for you. But it's what Amy wanted. You know that. Amy would have withered in one of these," I added, pointing to my wheelchair.

"I'll take you up there," he offered.

"That's not where I'm going, Jakob. I've already said goodbye to Amy."

"She told you about…us, about me, didn't she," he accused.

"She told me. That's all in the past. Amy loved you, Jakob. Don't make it anything less than that."

"I killed her!" he gritted. "I drove her out. That's how she got shot off that stump. And…I never helped her…afterwards. Not once! I kilt her! I done it!"

"Jakob, if you do anything but remember Amy as a wonderful girl who believed in her heart you were her lord and master, you're shaming her memory. What makes the difference? None of it make any difference. Just love her and remember her for what she was for you. You must not hate yourself, that would make her cry her heart out."

"How would you know?" he demanded suspiciously.

"Amy told me." I was getting used to telling whoppers.

"You going to drink that crazy man's poison?" he asked.

"I don't think I am."

"The Lord uses strange vessels for His work." Jakob was back to preaching.

"You're goin' up to her spring, ain't you, girl. Where she listened to them birds."

"That's where I'm going."

"I'll push you up, or carry you, for that matter."

"No. I want to be alone." I had a quick flashback of Jakob's problem with Amy in the washtub.

"Then go on, girl. It's near dark."

*   *   *

I labored up the long sandy trail toward Amy's spring. I had to stop twice, fighting total fatigue, shaking the wheelchair as I fought to get my breath. At the final stop before the shelter of the deep woods I twisted around and looked down the long sandy trail. The buggy was gone from the meeting yard.

Another fifty yards and I was at the edge of the huge spring feeding the grass-lined creek that spilled down the hillside far beyond the meeting house.

I sat by the soft music of the spring as twilight fell. The barest sliver of a new moon rose in the crease of the hollow ahead of me.

A huge doe stepped silently into the clearing, snapping her ears forward as she saw me, stamping her foot twice in disgust, then gave a harsh cough and spun back into the underbrush. Loud crashes followed as several animals fled. Then silence. Darkness gathered. My heart was sinking, I felt an overwhelming sense of hopelessness.

The whip-poor-will was so close it startled me. The plaintive call trilled into my ear. I looked into the gloom. It repeated loudly. *Whip-poor-Will...Whip-poor-Will...Whip-poor-Will!!*

Far up the ravine an answering call. A faint rustle, and I turned to see the small bird. Very compact and rounded, feathery whiskers surrounding its mouth; it looked sad and tired, like a tiny owl. Its bright eyes never left my face. It opened its throat and sang, shaking the tiny branch. I felt a shock pass down my entire body, my legs surged with thousands of sharp painful needle pricks, followed by a burning sensation...falling instantly to the dead vacuum that I had lived with from the moment of the crash. The bird flew silently, not the slightest sound as it disappeared into the dark ravine.

I crashed down the path as fast as the chair would go, careening dizzily, threatening to turn over or tear off into the thick underbrush. Fumbling with the remote, desperate to get the ramp down, I heard the song faintly in the distance.

"Amy," I whispered to myself, "I know. I hear you!"

I rolled up into the van and sped away toward Athens. Athens! Where Aesculapius walked. Where miracles happen! I wasn't making sense.

*   *   *

The car phone startled me as I sped down the dark road. I had forgotten the thing was in the van. It was Vince. "Toni?" he asked.

"Hello Vincent."

"Where the hell are you? I've been looking all over for you."

"I came up to the meeting house. I wanted to come up here for a bit."

"You're all right?"

"I'm fine. How's Dr. Scheckler?"

"Much better. We went out and had a steak. He refused to have anything to drink. Says he's over that. Toni, the keys to his lab are missing. You have them?"

"I took them to feed Priscilla."

"He said as much. You're coming here when you get to town?"

"Vince, it will be midnight. I'm going to sleep when I get there."

"See you in the morning then. We'll start back in the morning."

"See you then, Vincent."

LETHAL CONSEQUENCES

The street in front of the laboratory building was dark and silent. I parked, snapped off the lights and fought my way through the blackness to its heavy metal door. As I entered, Priscilla's soft overhead light greeted me. She stirred, gave an enormous yawn, then swayed lazily forward to watch me.

I hurried to the sink, this time taking down the largest beaker from the gleaming rack, balanced it carefully between my legs, concentrated on it as I wobbled past the steel and porcelain machines of modern science to Priscilla's refrigerator. I carefully removed the syringe, its needle and cap. I stretched up to the peg and took down the key.

Priscilla scuttled to the door and teetered back and forth, pushing off firmly with her huge knuckles, grasping her hands together like a huge praying mantis then falling forward again on all fours. As soon as I was inside, one blackened hand shot roughly between my legs, searching for and grasping the syringe. I swerved and teetered, fighting her for the syringe, trying to keep from losing the beaker from between my senseless legs while pumping awkwardly on the rubber wheel rim with whichever hand was free. She gripped the syringe like a vise and turned it over. As I pried it away from her she pulled back her lips and clicked her huge teeth viciously. I slammed the door before she could dart past me into the laboratory. That spun the chair crazily in the deep straw. Priscilla retreated to her favorite corner.

The chair wheels slipped unevenly as I hurried after her causing the beaker to roll down my thighs. I snatched it just before it bounced onto the hard metal of the footrests. By the time I made it to the back wall, Priscilla had loped to a new corner, her eyebrows darting up and down. Did she think this was some sort of a mad game? I was sweating and exhausted, clinging to the chair and panting. Priscilla raced around the room making groaning sounds. She perched again, as far away as the room allowed.

We sat and stared at each other. I reached down and flipped up the foot-rests, then slid forward out of the chair and pushed it away. It rolled several feet, then tipped over backwards. I pulled myself back against the wall, set the beaker carefully aside and used my arms to press myself up into a sitting position.

"Priscilla," I begged, "Look how strong you are. Just one little stick. Do this for me, Priscilla."

In the stillness only the refrigerator hummed. I watched her while she avoided my gaze and played games, sticking one finger after the other in her mouth and then examining the wetness. I rattled the syringe against the beaker. Twice. Very slowly and reluctantly she swung toward me, reproach in her eyes, settling beside me and presenting a huge bulging shoulder muscle. I quickly uncapped the needle, stuck it in the muscle and shot home the plunger. She slowly withdrew her arm and rubbed it. Then she grimaced and lay down beside me.

We lay there for four hours. I watched them creep past on my watch. Priscilla stirred occasionally, sometimes seemed to be dreaming. I dozed as well. Then Priscilla sneezed. I felt her forehead. It was warm and dry. She glared at me. An hour later she was feverish and miserable and her nose was running a constant stream. I collected her sneezes in the beaker, trying to keep from gagging as I collected every drop. At six thirty I crawled to the wheelchair, tilting it upright shakily as I protected the beaker. I worked my hand into the deep straw until I cleared a space on the cold cement, placed the beaker solidly, then grasped the chair and strained up over the seat, using all of my strength to sink down slowly and evenly. I leaned far over the side to retrieve the beaker. I forced my way crazily across the deep straw, the beaker wobbling alarmingly until I finally reached the hard surface of the lab floor. I slammed the door and hung up the key. Priscilla lay on the far wall moaning and sneezing.

I snatched the jug of orange juice from the refrigerator, and made my way to the sink. I returned and pulled out a tray of ice cubes. I stirred the slimy mess and placed it gingerly on the edge of Scheckler's desk then dumped in the ice cubes. I flipped open his notebook and strained to make some sense of the pages of scrawl. I tried the centrifuge, but when I snapped the switch the metal arms whirled out like steel snakes nearly smashing my hand. So I stirred the cubes vigorously, hoping the coldness might somehow help, and filtered it all through Scheckler's coffee apparatus. When the orange liquid filled a small beaker I took it with trembling hands, forced its cold surface against my neck with one hand while I steered clumsily for the door with the other.

I was a scarecrow in the early morning light, clothing covered with scraps of straw, the neckline and underarms of my filthy blouse dark with sweat. My hands were weak and sweaty as I clutched the beaker. Sunshine glinted and sparkled on the metal of the wheelchair. I extended my shaking arms toward the orange disk of sun barely breaking over the horizon and swallowed repeatedly trying to break the constriction in my throat.

"Amy," I said, peering at the bright orange liquid in the sunlight. I tilted it back and drank it down. A tiny bit ran from the corner of my mouth, I swiped at it with one hand, holding my breath desperately so I wouldn't vomit. The small beaker slipped wetly from my fingers, bounced away and smashed on the cement sidewalk. "Amy," I repeated softly, "I did it."

CONVULSION AND COMA

I forced myself back against the front wall of the laboratory and sat numbly, wondering about the virus sliding wickedly through my body, Scheckler said it was very fast didn't he? Was it streaking for my brain before anything could catch it and kill it? I shivered. The cold morning air penetrated my sweat-soaked blouse, the rising sun flooded the wall but I felt no heat. A passing car slowed, the passenger window drifted down and the driver leaned across to ask if I needed help. I waved him away. A scruffy dog paused and looked at me, wagging his tail to see if we should be buddies. Finally he gave up and trotted down the sidewalk. As my eye followed the dog, I saw figures running toward me, racing from Scheckler's motel. First was Vincent, running hard in his underwear. Scheckler was a block behind laboring in oversized black pajamas. I knew what had happened. Vincent had awakened, called the dorm room, when there was no answer he realized what *might* have happened, *had* happened; so now this foot race.

Vincent grabbed me by the shoulders and shook me. "Tell me this is a nightmare, Toni," he demanded. "*Tell me!*"

I pointed at the pieces of the beaker. "Ice cold orangutan snot and orange juice, Vincent. I can guarantee you it will never catch on at the Plaza."

I was swaying, wondering if I was going to faint. Vincent raced inside. Scheckler stumbled up, trying to talk to me and retie the frayed cord holding up his pajamas at the same time. He looked like a clown in a slapstick movie. Everything seemed very funny. I giggled, but it sounded like someone else giggling in the distance. Scheckler gave me an owl look below the heavy lids. He *knew* what I had done. I was sure of it.

"How much did you take?," he asked. He knew all right.

"All I could collect from the first sneeze until I couldn't stand it any longer."

"Did you prep yourself with the Cyclosporin A?"

"I did."

Scheckler gave me the faintest look of approval, then said, "Toni, you've ruined everything. This University, gene science, ten years of research. And you have probably committed suicide." He was amazingly calm.

"I don't believe that, and neither should you," I replied.

Vincent stomped out of the door. He took me by the elbow. "We're getting you out to the University airport," he said. "Barney begged a Gulfstream from Digital Equipment just as it was ready for a trip. He's soon in it and on his way here. You'll be in the Putnam by ten o'clock." He turned to Scheckler. "He says you're to come with us. He may end up wringing your neck, but I convinced him you might be useful." He turned and glared at me. I'm going to put you in the van," he scolded, "and we will go get your things." he squinted in the sun. "You feel sick?" He was really pissed. His concern about my being sick or not was cover-up. I felt like telling him that.

"Are you going into Wilson in your underwear, Vincent?" I asked nastily.

Antonelli glanced down at himself, finally grinned and said, "We'll go by my place first." He started to shove me toward the van.

"Call Cambridge," ordered Scheckler, sticking his head out of the door. "Get beta interferone. Tell them we want all they have."

∗   ∗   ∗

The University airfield was a small strip out on US 50. We waited in a stuffy room for an hour, it seemed too hot, but no-one else was complaining. The Gulfstream made two passes before the pilot decided to bring it in.

I remember Barney's tear-stained face. Then the whine of jet engines fading in and out and fragments of a terrible argument, mostly Barney's enraged voice. Much later there was a lot of jostling at Logan airport, the throb of a helicopter rising above the harbor. That was where I had a convulsion. The last thing I remember was Vincent stuffing something rigid in my mouth. I saw fear in his eyes. Nothing after that.

INTENSIVE CARE

White light wobbled. A fragment of face behind it, then blinding white light in my other eye. I squeezed my eyes shut.

"She's got pupillary reflexes," someone said. My eye was pried open and I was blinded again. "See?" said the voice.

My arms were strapped down at my sides. Someone, a nice soft female voice, spoke into my ear, "Take it easy! You're ok."

I opened my eyes. A huge brown rubber tube arched up out of my mouth. There was a machine-sound, like someone filling a tire, and I felt my chest fill up. Just before I exploded, it stopped and my chest sank back down with a long sighing sound. I fought to get my hands loose. The damn thing started to blow me up again. I tried to bite the tube but my mouth was stuffed full of some sort of cotton. "Whoa!" said the soft voice. "Don't fight. Let us do it.

You're fine." She apparently said that sort of thing all of the time.

"She's using her intercostals," said a male voice. I looked down past the tube and the tip of my nose. Two white-clad male adolescents were staring at my naked chest, like it was the deck of the Titanic.

"Yep," agreed the other. "Take it out."

There was painful fumbling around my mouth, tearing sensations across my forehead, followed by a delicate female hand pulling firmly on the brown tube which remained stubbornly in place until she gave it a sharp yank after which it began to slide slowly with the sensation that my lungs and throat were being ripped out with it. The end appeared with a collapsed dripping pale rubber sack flopping over it. I tried to say something but nothing happened.

"They've had you zonked for a week, Miss Putnam," the soft voice volunteered into my ear, "you know, amnesics, heavy sedation, so you didn't fight the respirator. You're fine," she repeated.

What she didn't know was that since the tube was out I was desperately trying to take a breath but nothing was happening. Panic was becoming terror. I was drowning. I was never going to breathe again.

"I dunno," said the youthful male voice, "she's starting to get a little blue."

"Just be patient," said the other. "When enough anoxia hits the medulla she'll take a breath."

The room light was turning brown and fuzzy. I twisted my upper body violently, trying to get my arms loose but I was fading into blackness. Just as the light winked out I took a huge breath and the lights brightened again. I took another quick one to be sure.

"See? I told you." said the second voice.

"Get a femoral stick in twenty minutes and if the oxygen saturation is above where we started, just keep an eye on her for an hour or so," the same voice ordered, now full of authority. "If it drops, give us a page, we'll re-intubate. Leave the respirator here. Get a fresh sterile endotracheal tube in here."

"Yes, sir," replied my comforter. So. Not a nurse, but a *student* nurse, still afraid of doctors! *She* was going to keep an eye on me to see if I was still breathing? She wouldn't call those two until I was bright purple.

She loosened my arms. I tried to again to speak but only croaked. Like something from a swamp. I turned my head. Barney and Jeanette were standing in front of the windows grinning and crying at the same time. They ran to me, bent over me, both talking. I grabbed for their clothing, anything I could find to hang onto. Barney finally pried my hands loose.

"This has been getting closer for two days, Toni," he said. They told us you were going to make it two days ago. They thought about weaning you off of the respirator yesterday, but decided to wait. We've never left the hospital for the past ten days." His heavily lined cheeks were coming into better focus. My mother smiled radiantly. A very beautiful woman. I tried to say something, but she put her fingertips on my lips.

"Don't try to say anything, Toni," she said. "Save your strength." Her eyes widened as she watched me. "Toni! What is it?" she demanded. She turned toward my father. "Look at her! What's she doing?"

I was trying desperately to talk but my throat was on fire. The nurse rushed over and pushed me back down on the bed, pressing the panic button on the pillow. I heard running feet. I still couldn't speak. I threshed at the covers and at the nurse. Several people ran in, including Vincent Antonelli.

"Toni, what is it?" he demanded.

"Scheckler," I croaked.

"What?"

"Scheckler." I sank back on the pillow exhausted. I couldn't get enough breath.

"She wants Dr. Scheckler," said my father, as calmly as if he was sitting in his office.

Vincent rushed out of the room. Another nurse came in with a syringe and needle and started to inject something into the IV tubing.

"No!" I croaked. "Don't knock me out! Get...Scheckler." She hesitated and Barney stepped forward and placed a hand on her arm.

"Let's wait a minute," he said.

Barney should have been a brain surgeon.

I lay there panting, watching all of them, particularly the nurse with the syringe. I heard Aaron Scheckler being paged. I closed my eyes.

There was a clatter in the hallway and Scheckler appeared, his eyes flashing over me, trying to understand what was wrong. He wore a white lab coat which had a large wet coffee stain down the front.

"What is it?" he demanded.

"You should know!" My voice cracked, but it was getting more reliable.

Scheckler looked back at my parents and then over at the two nurses, trying to understand. He shrugged his shoulders and opened out his hands like a card player accused of cheating. His black eyes gleamed from their deep sockets.

"Pull off the covers, Aaron," I said.

He took one of his halting careful steps, grasped the sheet and stripped it away. We stared at my legs.

"They burn like fire, Aaron," I said quietly. "And see, I can wiggle my toes." I wiggled them.

I wiggled them again causing a shower of pins and needles to shoot up my legs. They burned like they were being held over a bonfire.

There was a sibilant noise at the bedside, a soft hiss. Aaron Scheckler's eyes rolled back in his head, he repeated the hiss, then a low groan as he clutched clumsily at the sheet and fell heavily across my body. Then he flopped onto the floor. I was left naked, wiggling my toes.

THE MISTRESS OF THE VIRUS

They took me off to physical therapy every day, at first on a gurney, a week later in the wheelchair, and a month to the day after I was discharged from critical care, I walked down on my own. George paced at my side every step of the way, beaming at everyone as we passed, as if all of this was his doing, and mostly it was. I clutched at the nearby arm several times, it was the size of a tree trunk. I was still unsteady.

He had taken me from the gurney that first week and walked down into the pool with me in his massive arms, crying like a baby. The tears streamed down his cheeks as he looked down at me, completely unembarrassed by it. He floated me around in the warm water, getting a lot of advice from Vincent Antonelli, and Aaron Scheckler, and Coach Pearce…anyone, it seemed, who had nothing else to do. George mostly ignored what they said, and we floated where we pleased with him humming to himself. He encouraged me to move my legs, which at least once a day caused a series of sharp spasms, even nasty twisting cramps which would necessitate dragging me out of the water where they would massage my legs while I gritted my teeth and tried to act my age.

After several hours in the pool, George and Vince would take me to the exercise room where they placed me between the parallel bars and, suspended between the two muscle-men, I would take trembling steps. Then over to the electro-physiology lab where multiple needles were stuck into my skin and charts and graphs spewed out of machines while Scheckler and a crowd of residents and students huffed and puffed, looking over at me occasionally, I suppose to see if by chance I had been electrocuted.

Once back in my room there was always another long neurologic examination, finally something to eat. I was starved. I couldn't get enough. I begged Vincent to sneak in some pizza. He stared at me as if I had asked him if he was a male prostitute.

"Toni," he said in a tone reserved for idiots, "every milligram of your intake and output is measured and recorded. Your metabolism, muscle mass, urinary function, you name it, is costing small fortune to obtain every day. You want me to screw that up with pizza?"

"Let me near a piece and I'll show you."

"Forget it."

"You'll pay for this, Antonelli, I promise you. I know for sure that little boy who danced with me over in Davos would get me a pizza, no further questions asked."

"You seem to have that effect on a lot of men. George, for instance. But not me. The last time I trusted you, what did you do?"

"I made up a little after-midnight cocktail."

"Out of what?"

"Let's not get gross, Antonelli. Get out of here. If I can't get anything more to eat, I'm going to take a nap."

When I woke up the intense July afternoon sun was blazing at my windows, someone had lowered the Venetian blinds and there was a fiery line beneath each slat. Aaron Scheckler was riveted at my bedside as if I might disappear in a puff of smoke. I suppose his jerky movements were what awakened me. I sat up in bed and patted a spot beside me.

"There must be a band concert down at the basin, either that or you finally have a girlfriend. I've never seen you look so grand," I said to him. I brushed my hair back from where it had fallen across my face.

He sat gingerly beside me, facing toward me. He had on a new pin-striped black suit and a linen shirt with an open collar. Very sporty. He smiled his crooked smile.

"The secretary in the neurology lab took me up to Brooks Brothers," he admitted, "she said I was beginning to look like a homeless person."

"You're going to win the Nobel prize, Aaron, she wants to spruce you up," I said. He was fun to tease. He turned so many different colors.

He rubbed his chin with his thumb and a long skinny index finger.

"Toni, don't say that," he said. "Science doesn't work that way. There have to be reproducible results. From separate investigators. This could all be just a wonderful late spontaneous recovery…those thing happen, you know." He didn't look like he believed that at all.

"One of your neurologist friends came in yesterday with a student, Aaron. They gossiped while they examined me. He told her you were going to win the Nobel."

"That would be Austen," he replied. "Austen's a very positive thinker. Sometimes not all that scientific."

"He also said one or two more cases and you're going to have a line of wheelchairs that stretches from Athens clear to the Ohio River."

Aaron was uncomfortable. I didn't like it. I sensed this wasn't just a casual visit.

"What did you come here to tell me, Aaron," I asked. Small sparkles of fear started to run around in my head.

"Toni, do you know anything about a disease called multiple sclerosis," he asked.

"Practically nothing. I know Barney gives money to some sort of organization with that name. It sounds terrible." Fear was rising like a black volcano.

"It is a demyelinating disease. There's no treatment. It may go very slowly, or can go rapidly and…cause paralysis."

The volcano erupted. The room tilted and turned.

"Oh, God, Aaron, don't…."

He quickly raised his hand. "Toni, there's no evidence that you have this…problem. I just want to warn you that what has happened to you is all completely new. The messenger gene is in there and working for you every day. But…it could stop working. We just don't know. We have nothing to compare. Multiple sclerosis is the closest thing to any of this…"

I thought about this for a long time. I asked him to open the blinds so I could look at the Charles River sparkling in the sun.

"Whatever happens," I said finally, "I'm ready for it. I'm going to have a good life no matter what." I was trying very hard not to start bawling like a four-year-old.

He stood there, outlined by the bright light, a small figure, slightly stooped. "Toni, there's a lot of Amy Yoder in you," he said.

"I certainly hope so," I replied. "And Amy and I don't agree with you, Aaron. Amy and I are going to be just fine." I wondered if my chin was trembling the way hers did when she was scared the way I now was.

"There's more," said Scheckler.

"You bring a big load, don't you?" I never knew anyone who could irritate me as quickly as he could.

"I'm certain Priscilla is destroying the messenger virus. She's creating her own immunity. I asked them to inject her a week ago, and they called me from Athens today with the viral DNA titer. She's barely shedding virus at all. I've been expecting this."

"So what will happen to her?" I asked.

"Oh," said Scheckler happily, "she's going up to the Columbus Zoo. I told you once, a fine primate center. We've found a handsome male in San Diego who's going to visit. They call him Big Red. He weighs almost four hundred pounds." He grinned mischievously. "I'm sure Priscilla will like being a mother." He waited patiently, never doubting I would follow the track of his mind like a well trained mouse in a maze he had designed.

"So, you have no host for your virus. You can't treat anyone. Without Priscilla you can't get any virus for the next person. Without Priscilla, you're finished."

"Not quite."

It was sinking in. I swung my legs over the side of the bed to face him. He leaped up and backed away.

"Are you going to keep me in that little room with straw all over the floor and feed me oranges?" I asked.

I had to laugh. It wasn't a half-hearted laugh, or a scared laugh, it was really funny. Suddenly I felt wonderful.

An expression of immense relief flooded Aaron Scheckler's face. "It's not as bad as it sounds,Toni. You would have to be down there...in Athens...at a center they want to build. We would have to give you the injection, and you would...have symptoms, and the 'cold'. We'll have to keep you isolated until it's over...several days. They're ready to make the isolation suite at the O'Bleness Hospital if I give the word. This is no small undertaking. Ohio State University, Case Western Reserve, and , of course, the Putnam, are going to pitch in with the Osteopathic School at Ohio University. It'll be an enormous research effort. But it cannot move a fraction of an inch without you."

"Then tell them to get busy. Those viruses up in my brain are giving me an itch."

"Toni, it won't be forever that you'll do this. If we have another success, then we'll have another carrier, and over time, you'll also become immune and destroy the virus and no longer be a carrier or host."

"Then do I get a new four hundred pound boyfriend as a reward, Aaron? If so, you better tell Antonelli, he's promised to take me skiing when the first snow hits this autumn. He might be jealous."

"Antoinette Putnam, you're impossible. You're also the most brave and decent person I've ever known."

"Oh no, Dr. Scheckler, that was Amy."

He left me then. It was easy to see how delighted he was. I understood, with his massive pride, how difficult it had been for him to do what he had just done. As he marched out of the room there was less crouch and he held his head higher. Perhaps it was just the new suit. But what I really thought was that he was already practicing for the Nobel Prize.

THE WAGER AT
THE TOP OF THE MOUNTAIN

"I'll bet you I can beat you to the bottom," Vince shouted over the wind. "If I can't, I'll be your slave for life. If I win, I get to keep you all to myself for as long as I want."

"You mean until you get tired of me?"

"Something like that."

"Antonelli, you couldn't beat me to the bottom of Claim Jumper, let alone stand up on those black diamonds."

"I didn't plan to go that way." He stamped one ski on the snow. He had enough trouble getting off of the gondola. Now he was worried about his bindings.

We were standing in front of the Summit House at Park City. Ten thousand feet up in the winter sky with ice crystals swirling everywhere in the sunshine and the wind blowing snowy mares' tails off of the distant peaks. My favorite view in the whole world. Partly for the reason that I won my first big downhill here, but today because I'd never hoped to stand here again. I took it all in, then did a couple of deep knee bends. The thighs of steel were gone, Pearce and I found that out after two months of painful rehab, my racing days were over forever; but not my skiing days; and I was determined to make the most of every one of them.

Vincent was keeping a promise…to bring me here after the first big winter snowstorm, and it had hit just two days ago. We caught the evening flight out of Columbus for Salt Lake as soon as my classes at Ohio State finished yesterday afternoon. We were in line when the gondola lift opened this morning.

I was enrolled in the MBA program at the Fisher Business School. Twice in the past two months I had driven down to Athens where I was injected and isolated, with a contraption strapped to my nose to catch every drop. Then came the headache, the bone pain, the terrible fatigue and fever. I'm amazed Priscilla ever allowed me to inject her, knowing what was coming.

Finally, after what seemed an eternity, I would be medicated, and in two days back to something like normal. This had led to two incredibly successful treatments, and the peace and quiet of the Ohio University campus was now torn apart by bulldozers and giant cranes building the most advanced evaluation and treatment center for paralytic and demyelinating diseases in the world. Vincent was based in Cleveland, at the Cleveland Clinic where he had wrangled a residency in physical medicine, sports medicine, and rehabilitation. How he did that on short notice, I have no idea, but Antonelli could sell himself to Saint Peter in fifteen minutes if a pressing need arose.

Vince may have used the leverage of the paralysis project. Everyone wanted to help. There was a lot of publicity. While shopping in the supermarket I had the pleasure at the checkout counter of seeing my picture on a tabloid with headlines stating, "Ape girl has same blood type as her gorilla donor!" Of course they were wrong about the gorilla, but Priscilla and I do have the same blood type, as do many orangutans and humans. And Priscilla is an ape, for that matter, and I guess I'm now part ape if anyone wants to get technical about it. I bought a copy of the magazine and sent it to Jeanette.

Big Red is back in the San Diego Zoo; it was a brief liaison, and Priscilla is reported to be solidly pregnant, with her first ultra-sound scheduled in three weeks. I went up to the Columbus Zoo, they would not let me in her cage, but we touched each other through the bars, and she watched me standing in front of her, her head cocked slightly to one side with a marvelous expression of pleased comprehension.

"Toni!" exclaimed Antonelli, "Stop staring off into space! Better yet, let's go inside and get something hot, this wind is freezing!"

"You want to race to the bottom, or you want to sit around in some warming hut giving that toothy grin to some California blond?"

"Is the bet on?"

But I was over the lip and straight down the fall line. I let them run. The powder snow curled over the outside edge as I turned just far enough to see Vincent desperately trying to keep up. It was only a matter of time before he was going to be eating some serious snow. I was tempted to take it easy, even let him get ahead. As a matter of fact, I was curious if he would press his bet if he beat me.

I decided against that and tipped back to the vertical. I could feel my black braid thumping against the back of my neck, just like old times. After all, it wouldn't be right to let him win, would it? When red-tailed hawks are considering a mate, they fly up into the sun and tumble almost back to earth, there's no holding back. They don't fake it.

How do I know about something like that, I wondered? Then I remembered. I learned it from Amy. She told me as we sat together watching the evening sky several nights ago. Listening for the whip-poor-wills. In one of our dreams.